THE KEY'S BLIND SIDE

MICHAEL J. PIATT

Artwork By
Juan Giraldo

Dedicated to those who seek a better understanding through imagination.

TABLE OF CONTENTS

PROLOGUE

Under the rock atop Majestic Mountain lay a magic key carrying a peculiar and mysterious pull. It attracted those who dared uncover its secrets, for inscribed on its hidden side were the coordinates of a distant enchanted land. Even though the ancient inscription—painstakingly hand-chiseled—was well worn by the ages, one could clearly see the markings to be some sort of coordinates. They read twenty-one-*something* degrees latitude by seventy-*something* degrees longitude.

That mapped a place dead in the center of the Caribbean Islands—a sanctuary for derelict pirates and greedy thieves, who frequented it in hopes of the bountiful treasures aboard the billowing tall ships from centuries gone by.

The area was, in fact, almost directly on top of the islands designated by the pirates as their home base, a harbor of corruption.

But there was something more under that jagged rock—something that would set the course for an adventure into the past and beyond the imagination of the world of tomorrow.

It was a groove. That is correct; it was a simple groove, holding a key vertically, defying the sensations of gravity. The bizarrely harmonized forces of the universe supported it on its razor-sharp edge without any plausible explanation.

How did it get there and what was it for?

The former remains unknown; the latter is the makings of this epic adventure.

I

THE NEW THEATER PRODUCTION

The Sharefield Central High School students and the eclectic group of friends known as the Sharefield Gang were destined to bring the manuscript to life on their stage. Was it just the high school theater stage? Or was it the stage in which life itself plays out as the gang negotiates twists and turns embracing the inexplicable experiences of a lifetime.

The small-town Sharefield Gang of tenth-grade students was excited to participate in their new theater production, especially since last year's play was such a phenomenal success.

The gang was reluctant to participate back then until Kim convinced them otherwise. Unknown to any of them, this decision would change their lives forever. In the months to follow, over the summer break, many strange things started to happen.

In the most creepy and disturbing turn of events, the play began to transpire in their real lives!

One by one, the mystery behind those strange occurrences came to light, and the group was able to put together many pieces of the puzzle that confounded them.

Though some stubborn mysteries remained and carried forward into this new school year, the Sharefield Gang was hopeful this production of *The Caribbean Adventure* and the following events would reveal the truth from the previous year that defied explanation till the present.

Unfortunately, life got more challenging for the gang because the key had a blind side. A side that was not at all obvious at first encounter.

Chelsea was the seventh addition to the gang last school year after moving to Sharefield from another town. The other members, Dion, Nate, Kim, Lucia, Anthony, and Victor, unique in their own way, contributed to the Sharefield Gang's mystique. Their talents complemented each other, making them an inseparable group of friends. Their tenth-grade year promised to be even more exciting than last year as they ventured further into the unknown. It was to lead them to new discoveries beyond their wildest dreams.

This year's theater production was about events on a small Caribbean Island yet to be named. The theater director, Ms. Jill Brock, announced she would begin holding tryouts for the various parts the following week. The week prior, she invited interested students to walk with her through the basics of the production to better understand the storyline and to get a cursory view of the anticipated performance.

The Sharefield Gang was all in. During the first session, Ms. Brock orchestrated the production through descriptions and hand gestures. The more she described, the more it became apparent that the manuscript for this year's play had not been thoroughly vetted. It was as if Ms. Brock was improvising as she went along.

Production details seemed to change as days went by, and on Thursday of the first week, she admitted to everyone that some of the story points were still being developed. But she was confident that everyone would gather to make another fantastic production on the scale of last year's success.

"After all," she said, "Jimmy, the playwright of *The Caribbean Adventure*, has agreed to be directly involved with us to guide our representation of his work. I have arranged for everyone interested in participating to meet Jimmy after school on Friday afternoon before practice."

Kim said, "I have a question. Something has been bothering me since our school bonfire a couple weeks before school started. Brandon picked up some paper at the warehouse after our paper drive, and when he threw it on the fire to get it going, he realized it was a copy of last year's script. The one that Jimmy wrote. How did a copy end up there in the first place? We had been hunting for it for some time."

Ms. Brock furrowed her brows and replied, "I was not there that evening of the bonfire, but I heard about what happened. There must have been a misunderstanding. You see, I was getting ready for the new school year and cleaned out a lot of the old school paper near the end of your paper drive. I didn't have a chance to make it to the warehouse before it officially ended. Just after six o'clock that last Friday afternoon, I dropped off a couple boxes of paper at the door to the warehouse. A gentleman there said he would carry my boxes inside and store them with the rest of the material from your drive. There were several playbills from last year's production of *The Script* left over that I included in the recyclable material I took to the warehouse that evening. Since my boxes were in front of the other papers on the pallets, I assume that Brandon probably grabbed them. I suspect that the bundle of those playbills got thrown into the fire and burnt up, not the manuscript for which you were searching."

"Oh, that makes some sense," said Kim as realization dawned on her face. "Thank you!"

Ms. Brock commented, "Just wait till you meet Jimmy. He is quite talented in many respects."

The Sharefield Gang was eager to meet him because they had heard so much about him from their teacher. Jimmy was Ms. Brock's twin brother.

Nate walked into the theater room the next day and saw Lucia and Anthony already talking in the stage's corner.

Everyone else showed up within the next few minutes. Ms. Brock stood in the center of the stage as everyone gathered below her.

"I have a very special guest that I would like to introduce to all of you," she stated. "He will be helping us out this year with our production. In fact, he is the playwright that many of you have been waiting to meet. Allow me to introduce my brother. I always refer to him as Jimmy, and you should do the same because he likes to be informal. Everyone, say hello to Jimmy."

The gang did not know what to expect but figured he would come running out onto the stage. Nate knew Jimmy and Ms. Brock were twins, and he pictured him as a thin, tall man as energetic as his sister. After what seemed like an hour, although it was only a minute or so, he slowly emerged, wheeling himself out to the center of the stage. He looked a bit older than Ms. Brock, and his unkempt, bushy blond hair fell down on a face showing signs of a difficult past. When he began to speak, though, his voice was strong, upbeat, and dynamic, just like his sister's.

"Hello," said Jimmy. "I can hardly express to you just how elated and grateful I am to be a part of your renowned theater group for the presentation of *The Caribbean Adventure*." All eyes were on him as he spoke, as if to cross-examine him for authenticity.

Anthony immediately interjected, "Did you really write it yourself?"

"Well, yes," he answered, "but it is more like a work in progress. We will all have to collaborate to sort out some details."

When he ended his small speech, the students started chatting among themselves, not knowing what to make of this Jimmy guy. Nate, for one, who had a preconceived notion of what Jimmy would be like, now had to adjust his vision to the reality in front of him.

As the afternoon wore on, Jimmy and the classmates learned more about each other. The gang and the rest of the theater students quickly changed their opinions of Jimmy. Their first impression had been one of a man severely limited by his handicap, rendering him incapable of full engagement because he used a wheelchair. After getting to know him that afternoon, they all realized how wrong they were. Jimmy was a complex force that demanded their utmost respect. They already knew he was a botanist because Ms. Brock had told them about her brother, but he was so much more than that. He had traveled to many foreign lands and commanded knowledge of universal proportions on numerous worldly topics.

They also learned he was a lot like Ms. Brock in many ways, yet there were *some* differences. Jimmy seemed to bounce around from one topic to another in a haphazard manner. He seemed kind but not the sort of pleasant character that one immediately gravitates toward. He was more interested in facts and information than in expressing the human side of things. He openly admitted this, saying, "I need your help to make this play a totally immersive emotional experience for all who participate and come to see it."

This was the cue that Kim had been looking for. Ever since she received the gift of a gold pen last year from Arthur, the bus driver, she had been trying to figure out exactly why he had given it to her and why it had such significance. Now, things were becoming clearer. She felt like it was her purpose to help with the manuscript of this year's play.

Perhaps it's me, she thought, *who could change the production with the human elements necessary to touch the audience in a deeply emotional way, the same way people feel when they hold a newborn baby and see it smile.*

The thought of helping to script the play for her theater class resonated with her. Now in her mind was the question, *How will I approach Jimmy and Ms. Brock with this idea? After all*, she thought, *I am just a student about to try out for a part in the play, not at all a playwright.*

Yet, she somehow knew in her heart that the purpose behind the pen was to contribute to the production of *The Caribbean Adventure.*

Kim decided to wait a couple more days to see if Jimmy had anything more to say about the storyline and what the students made of it. As the days rolled off the calendar, the class began to bestow a certain authority on Jimmy's opinions. He was knowledgeable not only on many topics but also had an air about him. A certain confidence and passion for his art made everyone want to follow his every direction. This was the case, even if his often lack of focus made him different and, at times, difficult to follow.

The day before the official tryouts began, Dion summoned the courage to ask Jimmy about his wheelchair. "Jimmy, do you mind if I ask how you ended up in this wheelchair?"

In his most typical upbeat fashion, he responded, "No, not at all! I fell during a mountain climbing expedition several years ago, which left me paralyzed from my waist down. I must tell you the accident has made me stronger in many ways."

He did not need to explain any further. The students all understood; they were gazing at him in marvel, thinking they would want to have Jimmy by their side in any crisis.

Kim had told her classmates that she would really like to try her hand at creative writing and the word got around to Ms. Brock one day when she overheard some students talking before the theater session began.

She thought about the prospect of Kim helping Jimmy with the new manuscript, so that evening, Jill brought it up at a family dinner hosted by her parents. After listening to his sister, Jimmy thought it would be a great idea and would enjoy working with a young student who could add a fresh perspective. However, it was really their father who convinced her to give Kim the opportunity.

He told Jill, "Sometimes talent lies beneath the surface. You have an opportunity here to expose it."

Jill replied, "I can hardly say no to that."

So, on the first day of tryouts for the various parts in the production, Ms. Brock approached Kim and asked her if she wanted to collaborate with Jimmy on the manuscript rather than take a role as a cast member. Kim was ecstatic. She responded, saying, "This is a dream come true. Of course, I will do it!"

Jimmy then said to her, "I am impressed with your enthusiasm and thankful to have your help. I am confident you will add the missing dimensions to our production."

As the tryouts progressed the following week, the Sharefield Gang got into the swing of things. It was predetermined that Lucia would be doing all the costumes.

Ms. Brock told her, "Lucia, you did so well with the designs last year. We look forward to your magical creations of new, most colorful Caribbean designs to showcase this year's theme."

Nate told Anthony after all the cast members were announced, "I get to be Conta Nut, the wise old islander in search of his long-lost island heritage. It's what I was hoping I would get!"

Anthony replied, "I am Roger Jolly, the descendant of an actual pirate."

Chelsea, the newest member of the Sharefield Gang, tried out for and received the coveted role of the queen of the island.

Dion was given the role of Captain Fry. He thought to himself, *This character suits me. After what happened last summer on Majestic Mountain, I think I'd be perfect as the leader.*

Strangely, Victor did not show up on the second day of tryouts or the next day. His classmates remembered he came to school but was absent from theater practice later in the afternoon. The gang was concerned. This was not like him—Victor was always well-organized and prompt. He tended to always follow the rules.

The next morning, Dion ran into Victor between classes and asked, "Why haven't you been attending theater after school? We need you. The program is coming together, and you will want to secure your part."

Victor replied with an air of mystery, "Let's talk about it at lunchtime. I will see you then." He walked away.

Dion suspected something serious was going on. *Why couldn't he just give me a straight answer,* he thought. *Whatever it was, it was probably not good. Maybe he was ill or had decided to get involved in something different this year.*

When the last class of the morning ended, Dion gathered the rest of the gang and told them they all needed to sit together for lunch because Victor would explain why he was missing theater practice.

They all sat down, staring as if trying to pull an explanation out of his mouth.

Kim couldn't wait any longer and blurted out, "Victor, what's up? There has to be some logical explanation for why you have missed theater for two afternoons straight."

Victor had a look of bewilderment on his face. He wanted to come out and tell them, but his tongue would not cooperate. Instead, he reached over and hugged Kim right there at the table.

The friends exchanged nervous glances. Everyone knew then. Something wasn't right.

Lucia had a look of concern on her face. "Victor, what is it?"

He held his head low, and his voice shook as he muttered, "I am moving away."

"What?" Anthony cried out. "Did I hear you say what I thought you just said?"

"Yeah," said Victor. "My dad has been transferred. We are moving to the coast in just a few weeks."

Everyone was devastated.

"How could this be?" asked Dion. 'We have been friends in the Sharefield Gang since we started school. You cannot break us up."

"I know," Victor sighed. "My parents said it's definite, and I have no other options."

A tear sprung to Lucia's eyes as she whispered, "We will all miss you so much."

"I will miss you as well," said Victor, devastated. "We will always stay in touch with phone calls and messages."

"That is for sure," said Nate. "This will be a very difficult adjustment, my friend."

Chelsea said, "Victor, I have not known you as long as the others, but I feel like I have. This will leave a hole in our hearts."

Victor said, "We still have a few weeks together. Let's make the most of them. It'll be a new adventure for me. We all have people in our lives that come and leave. I guess that is just the way things are supposed to be."

Their lunch period was coming to an end. It was time for afternoon classes, so everyone stood silently and walked their separate ways toward their next class. They were reminiscing about the past and feeling the loss of a big part of their lives.

That evening, Nate called Victor and told him the entire Sharefield Gang would stay in touch despite many miles between them. There was not much more to be said. It was one of those times when words could not fill the void soon to be left by the departure of a best friend.

At Kim's insistence, Ms. Brock and Jimmy agreed to let Victor collaborate on completing the manuscript with them over the coming weeks before he left.

2

THE MANUSCRIPT

Kim was eager to begin working with Jimmy and Victor on the remaining dialog for the new school production. She always liked people and believed she had that emotional insight, sort of a sixth sense, to evoke feelings in others. *This performance would be the perfect opportunity for me to showcase that ability,* she thought. *It is exactly what Jimmy said was lacking.* She realized that Victor, so organized and logical, would be an irreplaceable asset to the project. Someone who could bring cohesiveness to the plot, a stark contrast to her occasional rambling.

The three met on the last day of tryouts to discuss what Jimmy had put together so far. He explained, "The events and sequences of this tale are all subject to change based upon your inputs."

This put Kim and Victor at ease. They felt empowered to make suggestions freely, knowing their input would be valued.

Jimmy continued, "The play will begin with the Sharefield City Council's decision to remove the mysterious key from its secure place for further examination. The local savings and loan bank kept it in a safety deposit box, so a council member would rather unceremoniously remove it soon after the bank opened one morning." Jimmy went on to describe in detail the story of *The Caribbean Adventure* as he had developed it to that point.

Upon close examination, there would be no obvious clues about its origin. It had no history, explanation of use, or identifying markings. At the next city council meeting, the members would decide that since this key was found near their local vicinity, it must have some bearing on the city's heritage. The town would organize a group of explorers to return to the top of Majestic Mountain, hoping to find clues about its mysterious past.

The volunteers set out early one morning to climb Majestic Mountain, anticipating what might be revealed to them on top of its highest peak. Brandon, and his friend Phillip, who supported the gang's expedition up Majestic Mountain last summer, were to make the journey with the others. They were also joined by several experienced adventure seekers.

After battling harsh conditions, the expedition team arrived at the summit by the end of the second day of hiking. It was nearly dark when they did, so the explorers began looking for the rock under which the key was found the first thing the following morning.

Brandon was up early with the sun and had already found the rock, aided by the description of where to look for it from the boys on the same mountain peak the previous summer. Brandon did not notice anything peculiar about this rock.

By this time, the others had gotten up and started looking around the area. Brandon showed everyone what he had found.

In accordance with the manuscript, Phillip said, "It looks like an ordinary rock to me. Funny that we came all the way up here to find a rock just like the ones in most of our backyards."

It was small enough to carry down the mountain, so Brandon said, "This is what we came up here to find. So, I will lug this thing down the mountain for others to examine further."

The expedition team spent the better part of that day looking around the top of the mountain for additional clues but came up with nothing of particular interest. They were not sure what they were looking for other than something that might relate to the mysterious key at the local bank.

When the team returned to Sharefield a day later, the rock Brandon found was presented to the city council members. Most of them just wanted to simply dismiss the project as frivolous. One member, Ms. Chang, was most interested in the rock and took it home to examine it more closely. After washing off the mud and scrubbing the rock with a bristle brush, she could see a groove at its bottom to support a key upright on its edge if laid down directly on top of it. Very interesting, she thought.

As she looked further, she could see there appeared to be an inscription on the stone. She removed a magnifying glass from her desk drawer and examined the rock further. With aided magnification, she spotted a message scribed in the stone. She could barely discern the letters and numbers through the glass as she adjusted its height above the rock. To her surprise, it read twenty-something degrees latitude by seventy-something degrees longitude. She ran to the globe on her desk and realized these coordinates were smack dab in the middle of the Caribbean Islands pirates frequented a couple hundred years ago.

Then she looked at the key again and realized it might open a treasure chest.

Jimmy finished narrating his story and said, "This is where I could use some of your expert assistance."

"Yes," Kim replied. "Ms. Chang needs to feel excitement and a bit of trepidation."

"That is perfect," said Jimmy. "I was trying to figure out what her reaction should be."

Kim nodded, "Yes, and it is the city council that would appropriately decide to visit the island to see if the mystery of the key can be solved."

"The voyage should be headed by Dion, as Captain Fry," suggested Victor.

Kim agreed and added, "I think that we should call the island Victorba in honor of you, Victor, our friend, who we will all miss very much."

Jimmy's eyes lit up. "That is a fine gesture and a good way to show tribute to a loyal friend. Allow me to continue."

Once the delegation arrives on the island of Victorba, they are greeted by Conta Nut, the elder wise man who runs the island's affairs. He tells the visitors stories of the island's past over his long lifetime on the island.

Kim interjected, "The stories he tells are of the island's abundant natural habitat for diverse species of plants and animals. He speaks of its thriving culture, with examples that are quite intriguing and inspirational to all. The island's people have prospered in recent times. Conta nut was a wise and just ruler."

Conta Nut stood tall above others, like a tree looking down with a watchful eye. He was hardheaded. His outer shell was tough, but inside, he was bittersweet. As he spoke, one could detect a hint of sadness in his voice despite all the success the island people had enjoyed under his guidance. Finally, he revealed that he did not know his own heritage. He was abandoned as a young boy and raised by a native family. Much of his adult life was spent trying to find out who his ancestors were. There was a hole in his heart. It matched all that he had of his past, a piece of a torn flag with an orange and black butterfly on it. He was wrapped in that flag when he was found by natives in the rainforest.

Conta Nut said he had searched the island high and low for clues that might shed some light on his past. Through all his investigations he had not come up with anything substantial. He referred to his ancestors, the early inhabitants of the islands before the Europeans came, as 'The Ancients.' The visitors from Sharefield were touched and decided to help him in his quest to understand his identity. They showed Conta Nut the special key and thought it might somehow be related to his past. Perhaps it was fate that brought them to the island to help him.

Conta Nut scanned the key and came to the same conclusion as the Sharefield visitors when they first saw it." It is a beautiful and well-crafted key," he noted. "Perhaps it is a key to a treasure chest left by pirates a few hundred years ago. I know of a descendant of the pirates living on this island. His name is Roger Jolly. I will be happy to introduce you to him if you would like. Maybe he knows something that would help you identify the meaning and the use of this most symbolic key."

3

THE SUNKEN SHIP

The following day, the delegation from the small town of Sharefield met Roger Jolly in person—a towering, muscular man. He told the captivating story of a sunken ship just off the coast of the island that was wedged in the coral reef. Few of the islanders knew of its existence. Legends surrounding the disaster claimed it had sunk in a battle over treasures at a time when pirates and vandals roamed the seas of the Caribbean. Roger had made it his hobby to dive down and explore the ship. Over the years he had trained himself to hold his breath underwater for several minutes.

"Very few people can do this," he spoke with a hint of pride in his gruff voice. "It is not something you would even want to *attempt without years of training." It was admirable that he did not use scuba gear and would freely dive down to the ship, look around for as long as he could, usually two or three minutes, and then carefully return to the surface to avoid injury.*

Roger spoke of the challenges of getting into the ship's hull and admitted he could only accomplish that feat on a few occasions.

"It takes extra stamina and just the right conditions to work my way inside the vessel and still get back up safely."

Over the years, Roger had discovered a few artifacts, which he proudly displayed for the delegation from Sharefield. The collection included a knife, several buttons, and a brass buckle. "I have never seen much of real value down there. These ships were often stripped down to bare crossbones so they could move quickly, powered by the brisk winds of the sea.

Then, in reflection, he mentioned, "You never know what you might find. Perhaps there is more to be discovered inside the ship if I could get more time underwater to investigate."

Roger told of how the coral in the reef had been deteriorating very rapidly over the past few years since he had been visiting the ship. It was losing all its color and turning a bleached white from small changes in the water temperature. He hoped these conditions could be reversed in time if the forces of nature somehow managed to rejuvenate it.

The Sharefield visitors were most intrigued by the stories of Roger Jolley. They knew this was their best chance to discover the story behind the key and agreed to arrange scuba equipment to be sent to the island of Victorba so that Roger could better explore the sunken ship.

To their surprise, Roger was not at all interested in the equipment. In fact, he told the guests there was already such equipment on the island.

"To me, ship diving is both a sport and a show of respect to my ancestors. They were pirates," he laughed. "I dare not cross them!" The truth was that diving was a sport he had trained for and had become quite proficient at. He wanted to continue his exploration as he had done for years. "I can stay underwater longer the more I go down there," he said. "I will make a special dive just to see if anything might relate to the key."

The Sharefield visitors were grateful to have his assistance.

On the first dive, Roger had some problems and needed to surface quickly after only a couple of minutes. He explained that he never really knows how well he will do under water before a dive. "Sometimes, I just don't have the lung capacity and need to cut things short." He agreed to wait a couple days to recover and then make a second attempt.

A few days later, Roger was feeling better. The weather conditions were perfect, and the sea was calm. The Sharefield visitors went out on the boat with Roger for the dive. That day, he had a more successful dive by several minutes. When he returned to the surface, he held something none of the visitors recognized. Once back on board the boat, Roger carefully examined his latest find. It was a set of rings resembling a globe mounted on a base. Roger told the others he knew what it was—an astrolabe.

He explained, "An instrument like this has been used since ancient times to determine location and time. It was commonly used by sailors to navigate the seas before the invention of the sextant and the compass."

It was quite a find and Roger was justifiably proud of it. He said an arrow was usually pointing upward at an angle through a center ball intended to represent the earth. Positioning the arrow properly toward the sun and stars and adjusting the rings accordingly gave a particularly good reading of the heavens. This included a determination of latitude.

"This astrolabe looks rather different than I would expect," he frowned.

The bottom part of an arrow was complete with fetching; the feathers found on the end of the arrow were intact, but the arrowhead was missing. In its place was a slotted bracket of some sort.

"This is very strange indeed," commented Roger. "In all the times I have been diving down to that ship, I have hardly found anything of interest. Then I found this astrolabe with a missing arrowhead. I do not know what to make of all of this."

The Sharefield guests were just as puzzled. One of them suggested that this strange astrolabe be shown to Conta Nut. Maybe he would have some answers.

Conta told the group that the astrolabe had revealed many things over the ages; it was a trusted instrument of The Ancients. He had a knack for looking at things from the inside out and a talent for putting things together that were seemingly unrelated. As soon as he saw the astrolabe, he remembered the key. *The end of a key is like an arrowhead that could point toward the stars,* he thought. He took the key and held it next to the astrolabe. He saw that the large end of the key would fit into the slot at the top of the astrolabe's arrow. He slid it into place, and almost instantly, it started to move.

As everyone looked on in wonder, the astrolabe took on a life of its own. All the rings began to swirl around on their axis in different directions, and the astrolabe rings spun under their own power, or one known only to the key. After a minute or so, they stopped.

"The positions of the rings provide directional coordinates," explained Roger.

He read the instrument carefully. Then exclaimed it was identifying a latitude very close to the island they were on, only one degree removed in the southern direction. The Sharefield visitors, still shocked by what they had just witnessed, asked what it meant.

Roger explained that the earth is divided into 360 degrees of latitude, so one degree is around sixty-nine miles in length. The astrolabe was pointing to a coordinate sixty-nine miles due south of their current location!

"What is down there?" asked one of the Sharefield delegation.

Conta Nut replied, "There is another island larger than Victorba located about that far away called Calustowa."

"That is very interesting," mused one of the visitors. "We must go there to continue our quest to understand this mysterious key."

Everyone agreed and immediately arranged to take a boat down to the next island. Conta insisted on going along, and so did Roger. The former had a feeling in his gut there may be something of particular interest to him down there.

"The investigation of the island of Calustowa is of utmost importance to all of us," said Conta Nut. "We must call upon our most talented explorer, Wanna Noah, to lead this expedition."

Jimmy interrupted, "Wanna Noah will be played by Barka, one of our best actresses on the stage, or so I am told. She has ambitions to become a professional on Broadway, and my sister believes she'll do the role justice. We have also selected Chelsea for the role of Hula Hope. I will introduce her now." He continued narrating the script.

Conta immediately contacted the queen of Calustowa, Hula Hope, and informed her of the pending visit. Hula was filled with positive energy and a strong belief in the future of the island. When they arrived, she met the visitors' boat at the dock and greeted them pleasantly. After listening intently to the entire story, she told the group of explorers they had free reign over the island to learn all they could about their mysterious calling to her island. Calustowa was considerably bigger than Victorba. The group decided it would be quite difficult to cover the entire island without some clues as to where to look, especially since no one knew exactly what they were looking for in the first place.

Once they got organized, Wanna Noah suggested they solicit a group of locals and ask them if anything strange had been happening on the island that might provide a clue.

"This way," nodded Kim, approval shining in her youthful eyes, "many more of the theater students will be able to dress up in traditional costumes to participate in the big meeting."

Jimmy was impressed with Kim's gesture to make sure everyone involved in the production had a part on stage, even if it was brief.

During that meeting, there was a lot of discussion over the key and considerable skepticism that it, along with the astrolabe it was attached to, somehow had mystical powers. Nonetheless, they all agreed in the end to help investigate the meaning behind this strange combination.

After several days of looking around the island of Calustowa, no one had turned up anything of interest; the local islanders were getting discouraged. Conta took the astrolabe and the accompanying key home with him that evening. As he stared at it from all sides and spun it around, he knew in his heart that it was special. Conta removed and replaced the key in the astrolabe, then watched it spin on its own once again. He knew it held the answers.

As it spun around, two of the small gems mounted at the base of the instrument fell out onto the table. Conta was surprised. He did not think this just happened by accident. This must mean something, he thought. After investigating the instrument with the missing gems for over an hour, he removed the key from the slot on top of the astrolabe.

He set the key down next to the gems, wondering what the significance between them could possibly be, and then he saw something. If he placed the gems on the key, one on each side of the center, they formed the eyes of what looked like a monkey's face engraved in the scrollwork of the center of the key. Amazing, he thought. He knew he had to ask the locals about monkeys on the island.

As fate would have it, there was a monkey sanctuary on the east side of the island that was restricted to visitors, allowing the monkey population to thrive and expand. Once Conta showed the key with the gems in place to the locals, everyone agreed this

was something worth exploring. Queen Hula Hope gave special access to the sanctuary to investigate the strange monkey face clue on the key.

On the first morning of discovery, the explorers saw monkeys of many different species frolicking around in their jungle habitat. They appeared happy to have the company of the visitors. As Roger Jolly, Conta, and the rest of the party walked among all the diverse exotic plant life, they saw nothing of particular interest related to the key. However, they were mesmerized by the beauty of the extraordinary plant life and the variety of thriving animal species.

Jimmy said, "I wanted to include something in the manuscript about the ecology of the Caribbean islands. The lovely people living on the islands have found many ingenious ways to utilize their resources over the centuries while preserving them. During my visit, I was struck by their ingenuity and creativity. I asked myself more than once, *How did they ever figure out so many things and then develop lasting traditions around them to preserve their environment? They were certainly not obvious when they were first discovered.*

The afternoon was a different story altogether. Soon after lunch, the group came across what looked to be a cave partially overgrown with vegetation. Roger had brought a large knife with him in case such an occasion arose and began cutting down some of the foliage to allow access to the cave. What appeared behind the vegetation was a cave flanked on both sides with large boulders. Conta ran up to the boulders as soon as they were revealed to him and gazed upon the inscriptions on the rocks leading to the entrance of the cave. On the right was a picture of a butterfly, but not just any butterfly. It was a monarch, like the one on the flag he had cherished since childhood.

On the opposite side was some writing describing an ancient island tribe residing here long before the European settlers. Conta knew he had located his people. Inside the cave they found further evidence and a couple artifacts that Conta would treasure forever. He was overjoyed to see he was a descendant of the tribe known as the Monarchies.

Upon their return, they once again met with Queen Hula Hope. Her head was spinning when they told her of their adventure on the island. "What comes around goes around," she said. "Everything is in a circle. Sometimes, you must round things out and even work against the gravity of the situation. There is a certain skill to it. You have acquired such a skill with this discovery. Now you will have the ability to explore spin-offs from this adventure."

No one really understood what she meant by that, but it did not matter. It was a time for celebration!

Victor suggested that a parade be included at this point in the play for all the cast and crew dressed in island attire.

"This would make a festive and colorful finale to our adventure!" he exclaimed.

Jimmy was impressed with the idea, so Kim wrote some dialog to incorporate the celebration. Chelsea's role in the play got more attractive as Kim continued to write it down. As the queen, she would be carried on a throne through the parade route around the stage.

The manuscript was complete, and the team of writers was satisfied. However, this created a challenge for Lucia. She needed to come up with many inexpensive costumes for everyone to participate in the parade while accurately reflecting the manuscript her friends had worked so hard to create.

She had the idea to make tie-dye T-shirts with the word *Calustowa* written on them. After all, this was the island of celebration. She checked out several other T-shirts with logos on them at the Sharefield Department Store. The logos felt like latex rubber to her. She got an idea that she thought would be worth a try. Maybe she could get some latex caulking, write the name on the shirts, and then do a standard tie-dye process after the caulking dried. Perhaps the dye would color the shirts, except where it was shielded by the latex writing. She decided to write on both the inside and the outside of the shirts as an extra precaution.

She made one shirt to see how it would turn out. It was perfect!

She had created a process for making custom tie-dye shirts and proceeded to make one for everyone—not only with the island name of Calustowa but also with each classmate's name on the back. Ms. Brock was truly impressed. She told each of the students that they could keep their shirts after the performance as a remembrance of the event. Although Victor would not be at the performance, Lucia also made a shirt for him so that he would have something to remember his contribution to the production.

The parade would include a steel drum with lots of dancing along the route. Roger Jolly, played by Anthony, was to be featured in the parade clowning around like he always does and presenting Chelsea, Queen Hula Hope, with their now-understood Key to the City. Or, in this case, the Key to the Island of Calustowa.

4

PRACTICING FOR PERFECTION

The class did not want to disappoint their teachers, parents, and friends, some of whom were also the authors of this play. So, just like last year, they set their sights high, striving to perform flawlessly. The casting was complete, and all responsibilities had been assigned. It was time to start practicing in earnest.

Unfortunately, it was becoming more difficult as the weather kept worsening. After-school theatre practice was canceled multiple times due to hazardous weather, and it didn't help that adequate transportation to get the students home after practice was not available. The problem got worse during a severe flu outbreak at the school, causing many students to stay home. Ms. Brock and Jimmy were justifiably concerned that the cast and crew would not have enough time to perfect their lines, dance routines, and scene changes. It looked like the entire production was in jeopardy! Every day, they watched helplessly as several critical members of the cast and crew regretfully dropped out, which disrupted the entire flow of the practice sessions.

Something had to be done.

Just what was expected of their favorite playwright, Jimmy had an idea. One rare day, when everyone was in attendance, he made a video of the entire performance and all the behind-the-scenes activities necessary for the performance's success. He made the video available to all the students involved so they could rehearse from the comfort of their own homes in case they were red-nosed and sniffling.

This was a compromise solution at best, but it was certainly better than nothing at all. The cast could rehearse their lines in sequence from the video with proper cues from the other actors.

As a new student, Chelsea wanted to make a favorable impression. It was also critical for her to perform well because she was the Queen of Calustowa. Since theater practice was canceled frequently, she tried to watch the video and learn her parts. One evening at dinner she complained to her father that it was particularly difficult for her to act out the scenes while trying to watch the video at the same time. Chelsea's dad hesitatingly offered her help. He might not be an actor or stage director, but he was a good father and would do whatever he could to help his only daughter.

His job involved research into new interactive technology. The company he worked for was developing glasses with built-in video capabilities to view whatever was in front of the wearer and identify the objects through artificial intelligence. The glasses had an integrated speaker so that whatever was recognized by the glasses would be spoken out loud. This development was being done in conjunction with an association for the visually impaired. The goal of the project was to provide the wearer with audio feedback on everything that was identified in front of them. The glasses, along with the associated software, would serve as eyes for those with impaired vision.

Thanks to his employer, he was able to get her a pair of virtual reality glasses for her birthday, which was coming up the following week.

When her father surprised her with them, she squealed with joy and felt privileged to have such advanced technology in the palm of her hands. While she stroked them, feeling the finishing in between her fingers, her dad explained that with this model of glasses, she could load the video of the school play rehearsal into them and watch. She did just that. After loading the video into the glasses, she practiced her lines and the dance routines at the same time. This was a much-improved solution. Through the special glasses, she felt like she was acting out the play with her classmates in real-time.

While she enjoyed most of it, there was one strange thing going on whenever she wore the glasses. It didn't bother her or interfere with her rehearsal, but it was a bit odd. The astrolabe with the key in it was always present in the lower right-hand field of view. Its arrow was spinning rather quickly, so one could not make out the details of the key, but it was clearly the same shape as the one used in the production. Chelsea didn't think too much of it. She figured it was just an error in the software because everything else about the glasses was fine.

After she told the others in the Sharefield Gang about this new approach, everyone wanted to try out the special glasses.

Chelsea was happy to share them with her friends. On days when they could not make it to the actual theater practice for one reason or another, they could now easily practice their lines and the choreographed routines put together by Ms. Brock. The glasses helped everyone in the gang as much as they did Chelsea. None of the others ever mentioned the astrolabe with the key in the lower right-hand field of view. Either they never noticed it, or it was somehow not present when they were using the glasses.

* * *

Time was fast approaching for Victor to say goodbye to his friends, and while everyone expected it, there was simply no easy way to do it. They were thankful for the last few weeks they spent together working on the production of *The Caribbean Adventure*.

It was fitting that the Sharefield Gang decided to meet in the park under their favorite oak tree to say their goodbyes. They had spent so much time there over the years that it had become a headquarters of sorts where they joined heads to handle the latest crisis at school or solve the world's problems.

They all met there directly after school on a Friday afternoon.

As they sat around in a circle, Kim said to Victor, "We have something for you to remember us by."

Victor immediately replied, "There was no need for that. I will never forget my Sharefield Gang friends, anyway."

"Neither will we," replied Kim, "but here is something for you to take along with you from all of us." She handed Victor a memory stick and said, "We've worked together to make this for you. It contains many of the pictures and videos of us over the years since the very beginnings of the Sharefield Gang."

Victor was touched. He said, "I will treasure this and think of it whenever I want to reconnect with all of you. This is the best gift that I could possibly receive from the gang."

Afterward, they all agreed to stay in touch. Then Victor shook his head, his expression pained, "I can't stay long. I told my parents that I would help them pack everything up for the long journey to the coast. We leave this weekend." He continued, "I have learned so much about dealing with the unknown through my friendship with all of you. You have helped prepare me for my next chapter. I see it as a new challenge thanks to what all of you have given to me. I'll never forget you."

On that tear-jerking note, they all said goodbye.

Victor had always sat in the same spot on the bus. That seat was left vacant from that day forward through the rest of the school year, in his memory.

* * *

Fortunately, everyone in the theater production was able to practice in person the last two weeks before the big event. Just like the year before, the play was a smashing success despite the difficulties getting time to practice together. Jimmy and Ms. Brock, along with Kim, got to sit back and watch the tenth-grade class outdo themselves with a stunning performance.

As scripted, near the end of the performance, the cast and the crew were honored in a parade through Calustowa to the beat of the steel drum. They were wearing the tie-dyed shirts that Lucia had so carefully crafted. Everyone looked fantastic. The entire theater class marched around the stage, waving and feeling the well-deserved pride swelling in their hearts. As they circled the audience, they received standing ovations from their friends and families.

Kim thought to herself, *It was worth all the hard work that I put into it.*

Lucia packed the shirt she'd dyed for Victor and sent it off to him the following day.

* * *

Kim wanted to do something special for Jimmy.

She said to Anthony and Lucia, "I want to thank Jimmy for the opportunity to explore my talent as a writer."

So, after much debate, Kim, Anthony, and Lucia decided to make him some cookies. According to Ms. Brock, oatmeal cookies were his favorite. They put them in a special canister that included a picture of Majestic Mountain from last year's production, along with the island of Calustowa. The canister was hand-drawn and painted by one of the very talented art students in the class. Everyone involved in the presentation signed the canister, even Victor, who was asked by Nate to forward his signature in a secure electronic form.

Once they had it all put together, the theater class met at the Mustang Pizza Restaurant in Sharefield one evening for the presentation.

Kim gave a short speech thanking Jimmy for all his support. She said, "You have demonstrated through example to everyone involved that we can accomplish incredible things if we remain committed and work as a team." She also noted that the theater participants, and she, in particular, learned not to judge someone by appearances or perceived impairments.

Jimmy was touched. He said, "I thank all of you students and my sister Jill for allowing me to be a part of the school theater program. I have learned a lot from you. I have come to realize just how powerful young minds are and how well they adapt to new technologies." He continued, "May these Cookies of Calustowa bring new insights to all at Central High. Without a doubt, you have the capacity and the will to accomplish phenomenal things. Our future is in good hands."

The students all cheered and clapped as Jimmy's small speech ended.

Then Dion asked Jimmy, "What do you plan to do next?"

He smiled and replied, "That has not been decided yet, but the influence of this experience with the students of Sharefield will stay with me forever."

5

VIRTUAL REALITY GLASSES

The Sharefield Gang decided to meet in the park on Saturday to hang out and relive the highlights of their theater production. For added engagement, Chelsea brought the virtual reality glasses that had helped her, and the others practice for the play when they could not be there in person. The gang was really intrigued with the glasses' capability. They took turns wearing them and going through the video of the play one last time. They laughed as they made up new lines on the spot, changing everything around. Still, no one mentioned the presence of the spinning astrolabe.

Dion said, "These glasses are so interesting. It'd be phenomenal if we could each get a pair of our own."

Anthony replied, "Yes, that *would* be fascinating. Just think what we could do with them!"

Kim responded, "We could create our own world and share it with each other."

Lucia exclaimed, "Just imagine all that we could create in such an artificial environment."

Last summer, the gang had agreed to save the money they earned cleaning up the old mansion on the hill. They had worked together on that project and thought that perhaps sometime in the future, they could each use the money they earned from Mr. and Ms. Martinez for something that they could all share together. Building a virtual world that they could all participate in seemed like the perfect motivation.

Chelsea and the entire gang were proud of her dad's work. They were hopeful they could get some version of the glasses and its software so they could experiment with them. Not to mention, they would have a lot of laughs just playing with them, especially if everyone had their own pair.

After a little coaxing from Chelsea, her dad agreed to suggest it to his company, and they decided to let the gang work with a slightly more advanced set of glasses. They loaned them to the students free of charge with the understanding that the gang would write a report on their findings regarding the experience after an evaluation period.

Chelsea shared the news with her friends.

Kim summed up their reaction, saying, "Wow, we all happily agree to that, of course."

The gang was ecstatic to have the chance to add value to this important development project, not to mention how much they would learn throughout the process.

As soon as the glasses were available, everyone met at Chelsea's house to pick up their pair and try them out. It was an exciting day!

The first time Anthony put on his glasses; he was looking around the living room at Chelsea's house. He said, "I can see everything perfectly." His glasses started naming everything in his field of vision. After a while, it began to frustrate Anthony. "Enough already," he muttered. "I can see everything here for myself."

Nate said, "I think that we're all going to have to learn how to adjust to these things. Once we do, we can make the most of them. Remember, Chelsea's dad was able to put a video of our theater performance into the memory of these glasses. Once we figure out how to do things like that for ourselves, we'll be off running in an artificial world that we can create and change however we like!"

"This all sounds so high-tech and thrilling at the same time!" cried Lucia.

Kim nodded. "We're limited only by our imagination. I love writing and want to help create a story for us in the glasses that'll be beyond our wildest dreams."

"Well, first we need to figure out how to do all these things," said Dion, struggling with the glasses on his face. "I agree with Anthony, listening to the glasses tell me what I'm already seeing is quite fascinating but also a little annoying."

Chelsea said, "I'll ask my dad how to turn off the object recognition speaker and how to upload and store video clips."

Lucia acknowledged, "Yes, if we can upload videos into the glasses, we can go around Sharefield and add scenes that we'd like to have as part of our virtual story."

The gang agreed to meet in Sharefield Park the following day and bring their glasses along in the hope that Chelsea would have an answer from her father by then.

When asked, Chelsea replied, "Dad said it's a simple procedure to set up the glasses the way you want without the audio for object recognition. After we set our glasses in the proper mode, we simply hit this first button here on the side of our glasses in the presence of the others. The software changes will automatically transfer to the other glasses in the vicinity with that one simple operation. Let's check it out."

Per her father's instructions, Chelsea hit the first button on her glasses. A green light flashed for a couple of seconds and then went off.

"I guess it is finished," she grinned, triumphant.

Dion put on his glasses as everyone watched in anticipatory silence.

"It must have worked," he said. "I don't hear anything."

After a short pause, the others followed suit. Everyone could see perfectly, and to their delight, there was no reporting of objects in their field of view.

"This is awesome," exclaimed Nate. "Now, how do we tell the glasses that we want to record what we're seeing, and how do we put these segments together and share them?"

Chelsea explained, "The ability to capture and record what the glasses are seeing is already built in. Dad showed me how. He said that when you want to record, you hit the second button on the side of the glasses. Then hit it again to stop the recording."

"That sounds simple enough," said Kim.

Chelsea continued, "To share recordings, we are supposed to touch the earpiece of our glasses with those of the others."

Anthony was thoroughly engaged and curious to experience the unknown. He declared, "Let's give it a try right now!"

He covered his eyes with the glasses and pressed the second button on their side as he saw a squirrel running up the trunk of a tree in front of him. Then, he pushed the same button again to stop the recording. After that, per Chelsea's instructions, he touched the earpiece of his glasses to those of each of his friends'.

"Now wear yours and tell me what you see," he said.

To everyone's amazement, they each saw the tree and the squirrel running up its trunk.

"We did it!" yelled Kim. "This is fantastic. Just imagine the immersive world we can create now. The possibilities are endless."

Anthony remarked, his voice all business now. "So now that we can go around collecting videos for our imaginary world, we need a way to edit it. We'll want to combine the segments in ways that'll make our world uniquely our own and mystifying beyond our wildest dreams."

Chelsea responded, "Tonight, I'll ask Dad about the next steps in the process."

Later that week, when the gang got together again, she happily reported that the glasses were equipped with some basic artificial intelligence that was being developed for another project.

"It can figure out on its own how to combine images and create circumstances based on audio input from its users. After collecting videos of our surroundings, all we have to do is wave our hand in front of the glasses and describe the situation we want to create in our virtual world. The intelligence in the glasses will take it from there and do the rest. It'll create circumstances based on the video and audio inputs that we provide."

The gang was in awe. This approach, most convincingly, simplified the challenge of creating a virtual world that was unique to the Sharefield Gang and easy for them to control.

Kim was especially eager to start collecting videos that could be used in the Sharefield Gang's virtual world. The friends agreed to meet in her basement one evening after school to discuss how that data would be collected among them and what they should call their new world.

Kim's basement was a place the gang all knew well. Over the years, ever since they were young, they've spent many hours down there playing games and dreaming of the future. It was a fitting place to explore the possibilities of their new virtual world.

As soon as everyone arrived at Kim's, Chelsea started off the discussion. "What should we call our new world, and what sorts of things are we going to do inside of it?" she asked.

Dion said, "Well, I would like for it to be a place to explore a new realm, domains outside of our comfort zone."

Nate agreed. "Yes, it should be a place of adventure that makes us question our conscious existence."

Then Lucia asked, "What will we call it? I was thinking, *The New World of Exploration*, but that sounds too childish."

Chelsea asked Anthony if he had any ideas.

He said, "I don't know. Maybe since we are going to collect video around our town of Sharefield we could call it *The Lost Field*, meaning things that are here but underneath the surface, not apparent to anyone but us."

Dion nodded. "It's simple, and it makes sense."

Lucia chimed in, "It's a field of view inside the glasses that we are talking about. Maybe we should call it *The Lost View*."

A faint appreciative murmur traveled through the gang that showed the name resonated with everyone, so the gang decided to stick with it.

"Welcome to the world of *The Lost View*!" announced Kim.

"Outstanding! Now we can get down to the business of importing video and images that'll become our new virtual world, *The Lost View*," Anthony said. "So, if I understand the instructions from Chelsea correctly, all we need to do is to go around Sharefield and record scenes of interest for our new world using the second button on the side of the glasses. After that we can all share the data with each other by touching the earpiece of the glasses together. From there on, all we have to do is wave our hand in front of the glasses and describe how we want the pieces to fit together in a given situation; then, the software does the rest for us. It'll create an artificial world that we can interact with."

Chelsea confirmed, "Yes, that's how my father explained it to me."

Dion was overwhelmed. He sighed, "There are so many visions running through my head. Where are the best places for us to record the video?"

Anthony had a suggestion. "First we should all record video of each other so that we can participate directly in our world rather than just being spectators."

"That is an excellent idea, Anthony; you are really thinking ahead. Sometimes you are amazing to me," grinned Lucia.

After recording all sorts of videos of each other with close-ups of facial expressions and action shots, they turned their attention to possible scenes for their virtual world.

Dion said, "We have all been drawn to water through our experiences on the Wandering River and its magnificent waterfalls. That is where we always get our class picture taken at the end of the school year. We should consider including it."

Nate said, "I'll go out there some day next week when the sun is shining and collect some video of the Wandering River falls that we are all so familiar with."

Lucia added, "I can go over to Lake Moon Glow, two miles downstream of the falls that are fed by the Wandering River. I should be able to get some interesting video there."

"Very good," said Kim, "we can divide up the town and the rest of the surrounding area in the same way. Each of us can collect video of different parts of it."

Chelsea interjected, "Once we have all the content, we can decide what to combine and share with each other."

Lucia suggested, "Let's wait to add the audio descriptions until everyone has shared their input so that we can decide as a group what sort of verbiage we want to associate with the various content."

All the friends were enthusiastic about this new adventure to collect videos of everything they could find of interest, both in Sharefield and all its beautiful natural surroundings. Within two weeks, everyone in the gang had a chance to visit their designated area and record what they found worthy.

The gang met again in Kim's basement one Saturday morning to share their input. Combining them into one huge database inside their glasses turned out to be a simple task. The amazing thing was, as they experimented with the glasses, they realized they could all view the same video-captured scene at the same time from whichever direction they happened to be facing.

"This is really cool," said Anthony. "Now let's input some information about our new world."

The gang let their imaginations run wild as they threw out ideas for their first virtual experience. It was Lucia who suggested that they key in on Lake Moon Glow.

"How about a boat?" asked Chelsea.

Nate said, "Since the lake is fed from the Wandering River, it makes me think of a tugboat moving through the river and entering the lake."

Kim smiled, "I like that idea. Let's call the boat *Tug*."

Nate, who had previously suggested using a video he collected of horses in the pasture, said, "It'd be both hilarious and challenging to have a horse race of some sort."

Chelsea remarked, "Don't forget, this is our world. We can do anything we like."

Dion frowned, "Yes, but we are now moving from a tugboat to a horse race. That is a bit of a stretch."

Anthony's eyes lit up with an idea. "Why don't we each ride a seahorse and race in an oval track on the lake around Tug, in the center."

"That sounds pretty cool," cooed Chelsea. Everyone else agreed, too. So, she waved her hand in front of her glasses, even though she was not wearing them at the time and started to describe the seahorses that could race around a boat called Tug on Lake Moon Glow. Each member of the gang followed by inputting preferences for their seahorse's color and its characteristics.

Anthony suggested, "We need to all come up with names for our seahorses."

Lucia said, "I name my beautiful, brownish-red seahorse Water Chestnut."

Nate chimed in, "My seahorse shall be called Clyde Sail."

"I choose Sea Biscotti," laughed Chelsea.

Dion said with mock solemnity, "My horse will be known as Ski Dattle, and you guys better watch out, he is fast."

Kim thought for a moment. "I'm going to go with something like Water Equestrian. I know! How about Aquastrian?"

Anthony said, "Wow, you have all chosen incredible names."

"You haven't chosen a name for yours, Anthony!" urged Lucia.

"OK, OK," said Anthony. "I will go with Poky Hokey Dokey."

Everyone laughed.

"That is Anthony for you," said Nate. "The name is a little long."

Anthony shrugged. "I will just call him Poky for short."

"What a successful start for the world of *The Lost View*," said Chelsea.

"I wonder what it looks like," mused Kim.

"There's only one way to find out," offered Dion.

Everyone put on their glasses to take a look around their new world. To their utter amazement, they were all looking at Lake Moon Glow. In the center of the lake was a white and red tugboat with the name *TUG* prominently displayed on the back transom of the boat. Tied up to its side were the reins of six large seahorses floating above the water. Each of them appeared precisely as their new owner described them. They were saddled up and ready to ride.

The Sharefield Gang was elated! Even though the new world looked tempting, they needed time to process what they were about to experience. Besides, it was getting late and there was not sufficient time to really immerse themselves in their new world that afternoon. They all agreed to get together the following Monday after school in Kim's basement to begin their adventure in *The Lost View*.

Time passed slowly as they anxiously awaited their first interactive session, and then, the day finally came. As everyone arrived at Kim's and prepared to put on their glasses, she remarked, "This is exciting and also a little bit intimidating."

"I know what you mean," Chelsea's big eyes widened. "We don't know where this is going to lead us, but it will be an exciting ride, that I know for sure."

Dion smiled. "This reminds me of the start of our climb up Majestic Mountain last summer. You know you are about to face the unknown. Somehow, puts both a smile on your face and butterflies in your stomach."

Nate commented, "Maybe that is what discovery is all about."

"OK, enough with the talk, let's do this." Anthony rubbed his hands.

And with that, the Sharefield Gang all put on their glasses to begin a wild new adventure. Immediately, they were all looking out over Lake Moon Glow at their boat, Tug, situated in the center of the lake with the six seahorses. No one was quite sure what to do next.

Remembering the instructions from her father, Chelsea said, "Dad told me to wave my hand in front of the glasses one time and then say what I want to control in the artificial world."

"Let's give it a try then," said Lucia. She waved her hand across the front of her glasses and said, "I am sitting on Water Chestnut."

Instantly, everyone saw through their glasses the spitting image of Lucia out in the middle of Lake Moon Glow, sitting on her chestnut-colored seahorse. Not wanting to be left behind, each of the others waved their hands in front of their glasses and stated that they were seated on their own horses.

Before they knew it, they were all looking at each other over the top of their seahorse's head.

"This is too much," said Anthony.

Just then, Nate covered his mouth with his hand and said, "I'm going to sneeze." As he did, his hand waved over his glasses, signaling the world of *The Lost View* to respond. The others saw him sneeze through their glasses as Clyde Sail reared up and would have thrown him off the back of the saddle had he not been holding the reins so tightly. "Wow, that was a close one," he sniffed.

As it turned out, Chelsea was the only one in the group who had ridden a horse before. Her dad had given her riding lessons as a young girl, so she knew it was going to take a little training before the others could ride comfortably. She told her friends to take their reins and follow her, single file, in a slow trot, or swim, in this case, around Tug.

"Pull to the left, and your seahorse goes left; pull to the right, and it will go in that direction," she instructed. "Pull back on the reins to make it stop and tap it on the sides with your feet to speed up your trusty long-tailed friend. This is roughly how they have been trained. Once you ride for a while you'll get more of a feel of how your own seahorse responds to your commands."

Chelsea slowly led her friends around Tug a couple of times and then ventured out farther into the lake. Everyone followed closely behind her in a single file.

Lucia said, "I keep getting the feeling that I'm going to fall off of Water Chestnut."

"That's common," said Chelsea, "just keep hold of the reins. Your thoroughbred won't let you down."

After about fifteen minutes or so, everyone seemed to get the hang of it, so she increased her pace. Within an hour, the gang was gliding across the lake with the greatest of ease, negotiating shark-like turns on their trusty sea mounts and stopping them on a dime's worth of lake water.

"We're ready to race," declared Kim.

Anthony added in agreement, "Poky Hokey Dokey and I are a rocking seahorse combination."

Even though the gang was ready to go, they decided to end their first real interactive session in the world of *The Lost View* and get back to reality since they each had homework and other responsibilities that evening.

The gang planned to re-enter their virtual world on the weekend when they'd have enough time to experience the joy of their first seahorse race.

6

TUG-OF-WAR

The following afternoon, as decided, the gang all showed up at Kim's house and headed directly to her basement for their second exhilarating adventure in the world of *The Lost View*. As they put on their glasses, they saw Tug sitting calmly by himself in the middle of Lake Moon Glow.

"Have the seahorses run off somewhere?" asked Dion, squinting into the distance.

"Perhaps they sensed our race was about to happen next and hid," replied Anthony.

All of a sudden, the sky above Lake Moon Glow turned dark and cloudy, and the wind picked up, making waves crash against the tall grass surrounding the lake. The grass bent over to the ground against the combined forces of the wind and the waves. Tug swayed back and forth in the high seas of the lake, steadily taking on the waves with each sway. The gang could see a silhouette in the distance gliding down the Wandering River toward the opening into Lake Moon Glow. It was partially dark from the clouds above, making it hard to see exactly what it was.

"What in the world, imaginary or otherwise, could that thing be?" asked Kim in a wondering, frightful voice.

Lucia gulped. "I don't know, but it doesn't look friendly."

As it moved into the lake, it turned to its side. The gang hurried to take a better look at it.

Dion said, "It looks like a vessel of some sort. I can't quite make out the details."

As it advanced into the lake, Anthony exclaimed, "Holy gold shillings, it is a pirate's vessel, I think!"

Nate whispered, "It looks like it could be an evil tugboat."

Indeed, it was. It had come to challenge Tug for control of Lake Moon Glow. The seahorses, sensing the danger, had all hidden along the south side of the shore.

Chelsea spotted them all huddled together in one spot.

As the strange vessel approached Tug, the gang read the name on the side of the mysterious pirate boat.

It says, "Deep Dungeon!" exclaimed Dion.

After sitting next to Tug for several minutes, evidently engaged in obscure conversation, Tug announced that Deep Dungeon was named for its disgusting galley. It had challenged the Sharefield Gang's Tug to an all-out tug-of-war game for full control of Lake Moon Glow.

Chelsea said, "Wait a minute, this isn't something we scripted at all. The world of *The Lost View* seems to be acting like it has a mind of its own. What's going on here?"

Just as she finished speaking, the two boats with an attached thick, heavy rope between them began to advance in opposite directions. The rope began to tighten as the two seaworthy vessels slowly trolled farther apart. As the rope tautened further, both drove forward at full throttle. It became a vicious battle. The war went on for nearly two hours, back and forth, as the gang watched in agonizing suspense.

Deep Dungeon was blowing black smoke into the air as high as one could see, blocking the sun and forming a particularly dark cloud over the lake. Tug dug his rotor in deep against the Dungeon, who was well known among pirate tugboats for his dual motors strategically located on each side of the boat for added stability.

There was a burst of jubilation from the gang every time Tug made an advance, only to be followed by screams of desperation when he lost ground to his rival. The two boats were so evenly matched that neither one could maintain an advantage over the other for a long period.

As the competition wore on, Tug started running low on fuel. If he ran out before Deep Dungeon, that would most certainly spell defeat for the gang's Tug. It looked like defeat was on the horizon as Deep Dungeon approached his shoreline.

While the gang focused on the battle in front of them, Chelsea happened to notice something peculiar. There was an image of a key in her lower right-hand view. It appeared to be the same one used in the school theater production of *The Caribbean Adventure*. She could not tell for sure because it was spinning around on its tip like a tightly wound old-fashioned top just released from its string. The key was not attached to the astrolabe as it had been when she first saw it in the video of the school theater production. This time, it was just the key spinning by itself. She wondered if the others could see it. She said, "Does anyone else see a spinning key in the lower right of their field of view?"

"Yes, I see it," said Nate.

"Oh, I see it also," said Kim.

Everyone else confirmed, too.

"What is it doing here?" Nate asked. "And why is it spinning?"

"How did it ever get into our virtual world in the first place?" Anthony wondered out loud.

Kim admitted, "I took a picture of the key and added it to my data for good luck, but why is it showing up now?"

It had no apparent relationship to anything else going on in the world of *The Lost View* at this critical time amid the life-or-death tug-of-war competition.

Then, suddenly, there was a sharp snapping sound. It echoed across the lake like the crack of a whip. The rope between Tug and Deep Dungeon, which had begun to fray in the middle, broke in two just as Tug gave his last pull out of sheer desperation. The very last drop of gasoline pumped from his depleted gas tank, causing Tug's motor to stall as he silently coasted into the middle of the lake. He was out of fuel, but boy, was he fuming mad. The Sharefield Gang's little boat was visually upset. He was throwing a 'tug tantrum' and taking on water as he swayed from side to side.

The circumstances were quite different for Deep Dungeon. That vengeful vessel went flying and crashed into a huge boulder on the edge of the lake. It sounded like branches from an entire forest of trees snapping in two at the same time. Deep Dungeon broke into a thousand pieces as he threw scraps of wood onto the shore and back into the lake toward his enemy. One large chunk of the pirate vessel hull just missed Tug off the starboard side.

Most interestingly, the force of the impact of Deep Dungeon against the hard granite rock released a sharp piece of wood in the form of an arrow that drove itself right through the flag atop Tug, who sat silently in the middle of the lake. It was lodged in the torn flag like the show of a hero who won the battle but suffered significant losses.

It was a close call, but Tug was victorious and remained in control of Lake Moon Glow for the foreseeable future, and the Sharefield Gang was most thankful for that.

The gang thought it had come to an end, and were about to erupt in cheers when something even stranger happened next. The cloud of debris mixed with all the black smoke from Deep Dungeon had an odd and pungent odor, almost like the smell of sulfur and rotten eggs. The weirdest thing was that the gang could all smell it. It was not in their virtual world but in their real one as well. The smell was as rancid as it could be.

But seeing Tug in his brutal form, the friends forgot about the smell and decided to tend to their boat.

Tug had suffered some damage that would require considerable craftsmanship to repair. Chelsea waved her hand in front of her glasses and asked for a boat restoration specialist, but no one appeared. Then she remembered what her father had previously explained to her in one of their general discussions about artificial intelligence: that the latest artificial intelligence systems could create fictitious characters and situations. Events could even be partially manipulated in real time with input from users.

No matter how advanced it was, it was incapable of creating human subjects out of thin air. Generating all the complexities of an actual human being without further input was beyond its capabilities. No such real person had been input by the gang prior to creating their artificial world.

They were just going to have to repair the vessel themselves. Lucia waved her hand in front of her glasses and spoke of boat repair equipment. All that appeared was a large package of silver-blueish-looking screws that shone in the bright afternoon sun, which somehow reappeared right after the evil boat's demise. So much so that one could hardly look straight at them.

"Well, we're going to have to figure this out ourselves," Lucia sighed. She took one of the screws and touched the head of it with her index finger. It began to spin in her hand. "I get it," she said. "We just place these screws in the correct location on Tug and then touch them with our finger to screw them into the wood."

"Very cool!" said Kim.

Now that Deep Dungeon was gone, the seahorses had nothing to fear anymore. They hopped out from their hiding spot, eager to be ridden.

Anthony gently jumped on Poky, glided over to Tug, and threw a line over the bow. He slowly pulled the limping Tug to the shoreline, where the gang gathered around to inspect the damage. Evidently, when the rope broke, it caught the rear side corner of the vessel and tore a piece of wood loose. Tug's steering rudder was also damaged.

Dion observed, "This is a lot like inventing. We must figure this out without an instruction manual."

Nate nodded confidently. "We can do it. We have plenty of these screws, let's just start putting them in and see how it goes."

Just for practice, Chelsea grabbed a screw and tried to screw it into a branch on the shore next to Lake Moon Glow. As her finger touched the head of the screw, it began to turn and grabbed into the bark of the branch. Then it went crooked and quickly screwed itself deep into the branch at an angle. It penetrated so fast that the wood began to smoke.

"Wow," said Anthony. "These things are powerful."

"Let me try one," said Lucia. She gently touched her finger to the screw and removed it as it started to accelerate into the branch. It went in straight and stopped as the head of the screw secured itself into the outer bark of the tree.

Dion was watching. He observed, "We just have to take it easy with these things. They require a light touch."

Kim nodded in appreciation, saying "We can handle this."

The gang proceeded to place the loose and broken parts back together like a puzzle, gently attaching each one with a line of screws. Tug started to look like he had been stitched back together with a needle and thread.

The repairs turned out to be simple enough for the gang, but the broken rudder was proving itself to be quite a bit trickier to manage.

Dion said, "We're going to have to get the back end of Tug up out of the water to fix this rudder."

Anthony found a huge log near the shore. Together, the six friends rolled the massive log into the water. Then they instructed Tug to slowly drive up right over the top of it and then stop.

"Wait a minute," said Nate. "First we need to switch Tug over to his reserve fuel tank." He proceeded to do just that.

Then Kim instructed Tug, "Slowly ride up over the log and stop about halfway."

Understanding every word the girl said to him, Tug did exactly what was asked of him and stopped just at the right spot leaving his back end suspended up in the air. Nate got into the water and repaired the cracked rudder with a few added screws. "Everything is looking good," he smiled. "Now all we have to do is get Tug back off this floating log."

The gang all yelled for him to move but he couldn't go forward or in reverse. He was stuck on the log with his prop up in the air.

"We need an idea to get Tug off of this log," Kim said. "Instead of trying to raise him, maybe we can sink the log down far enough to allow Tug to move himself off the log," suggested Nate.

"That is excellent reverse thinking!" said Chelsea.

The gang divided themselves into two groups. Three of them sat on the huge log on each side of Tug, allowing it to sink under the water just far enough for Tug's propeller to set on the surface of the water. He applied full throttle in reverse. His prop on the surface was throwing water halfway across the lake as his bow slowly began to slide off the log. Then he scraped across a knot in the log and stopped moving. He was stuck again.

The gang groaned in frustration.

Dion had an idea. He instructed everyone, "Let's bounce up and down together. On three, everybody get up, and I will call out our rhythm. One, two, three; up, down, up, down."

The gang started bouncing up and down on the massive log in unison.

Dion repeated this six times. Each time the log moved downward with the motion of the gang, Tug backed off the log a little farther. After half a dozen tries, Tug was free of the log and flying across the lake in reverse at full throttle.

Tug stopped, reversed direction, then moved forward and did a test run around the lake, speeding past the gang and splashing them all with water out of jubilation.

It was his way of showing his appreciation.

Tug was as good as new, and all was well.

The friends took off their glasses. They were extremely impressed with the world they had created with the power of artificial intelligence.

Chelsea said, "This is enough for me for one day. I am absolutely amazed and exhausted at the same time."

The rest of the gang felt the same way. This was an incredible and realistic experience, but now everyone knew that they needed to focus on their schoolwork.

The Sharefield Gang agreed to meet again the following weekend to experience whatever adventure awaited them next in their fantasy world.

The rest of the week went by quickly as the gang anticipated another unpredictable adventure.

Chelsea made a point of telling her father just how much she and her friends were amused with this virtual world.

"It is all pretty exciting," she exclaimed to her father as she ran through the account of the tug-of-war competition. She also told him that she didn't expect the glasses would have so much capability.

The system had gone off and fabricated this detailed, entertaining tug-of-war adventure on its own.

Chelsea's dad frowned but said, "These systems are getting more powerful with each passing day."

He didn't want Chelsea to see his apprehension. Secretly, he was astonished by the artificial intelligence's performance and rather concerned that there had somehow been a mistake.

Chelsea asked her dad, "Why do you suppose the image of the spinning key that Kim had added was visible in the lower right-hand corner during the tug-of-war competition?" He replied, "That's an interesting question. I have no idea."

There is something about this software that is just not quite right, he thought. The weekend arrived rather quickly, and the gang agreed to meet in Kim's basement on Saturday morning to continue their adventure. Everyone was there by ten in the morning, ready to experience whatever was to come next.

As they each picked up their glasses, Chelsea said once again, "We don't know where this is going to lead us, but it'll surely be an exciting ride."

"Hear, hear," she heard her friends' chorus.

7

GREEN SLIME

They placed the glasses over their eyes, expecting to see Tug and their seahorses resting comfortably in the middle of Lake Moon Glow.

To their utter horror and surprise, the lake was completely covered with slimy green-looking stuff resembling icing on a cake, only gross. Tug was covered up to his deck in this unusual substance. The poor seahorses were also head to tail in green goop. They stood motionless next to Tug. It was a dreadful sight.

Anthony said, "Oh, I hope my Poky Hokey Dokey is OK. The green ganache has got him by the tail."

Chelsea was worried. "My Sea Biscotti is not moving; this could be big trouble."

The gang continued to look on in silence for what seemed an eternity, but there was no movement at all on the lake. It was as if they were viewing a frozen picture.

Finally, Kim broke the silence, saying, "Contamination from Deep Dungeon must have poisoned our beautiful lake."

Then Dion noticed the spinning key had appeared once again in the lower right hand of their view. He pointed it out to the others. They all saw it.

Finally, after several more minutes, Kim noticed that Aquastrian was wiggling his tail and moving from side to side. "What a welcoming sight," she said.

"We need to do something," urged Dion.

"Yes, for sure," said Nate, "but what can we do to fix this problem?"

Anthony only shook his head. "I have no idea."

Chelsea suggested, "Well, maybe we don't need to solve this problem. Maybe the artificial intelligence that created it in the first place can figure it out." She waved her hand in front of her glasses, saying, "We want to dissolve the green slime covering Lake Moon Glow."

Everyone concentrated as they waited for something exciting to happen, but nothing did. Then, out of the corner of her eye, Lucia noticed what appeared to be a small lizard along the side of the lake near where Deep Dungeon had crashed. It dipped its head into the water as if to take a drink. She pointed it out to the rest of the gang.

"Well, I hope he likes the green stuff!" Anthony laughed.

It didn't appear that anything was going to fix the green slime. The gang was terribly disappointed. There was nothing else interesting going on, so they decided to quit for the day and get some physical exercise. They all realized that temporarily moving away from a problem and engaging in physical activity was a good way to help generate creative inspiration. That green slime was figuratively getting under their skin.

They headed off to the park in hopes of playing a little soccer with a group that usually met there on the weekends. Sure enough, they ran into several of their classmates at the park. The gang all enjoyed an afternoon of soccer, alternating in and out from one team to another. Nate was by far the best; soccer was his game. Everyone wanted him on their team because he consistently scored goals in every game he played.

The next time the gang was free to revisit their world of *The Lost View* was the following Wednesday. When they put on their glasses that evening after school, what they saw was even more bizarre than the disgusting green slime they had run away from.

A large prehistoric dragon-looking creature was jumping in and out of the water like a dolphin in the sea. It appeared to be eating the green slime as it maneuvered through the lake. In fact, the water near the Deep Dungeon crash site was completely clear.

Lucia said, "You don't suppose our dragon is eating up all this green stuff and growing like a weed, so to speak?"

Kim shrugged. "Well, I guess it's possible."

"Maybe Chelsea's request has been answered," grinned Dion.

The gang was not about to get on their seahorses, or Tug for that matter, with that creature swarming in the area. They decided to go up the Wandering River that fed Lake Moon Glow to check it out. As they walked along, they could see that the green slime had spread all the way up to the river.

After they hiked a couple miles, the river started to clear. Its color turned more of a faded green. The gang decided it might be invigorating to ride the river back down to the lake.

Anthony said, "Let's try a little green water rafting, I am game!"

Everyone agreed it would be an interesting experience. Kim waved her hand in front of her glasses and said, "We need a raft."

With that, there appeared a fully inflated raft spacious enough to hold the six of them. They all jumped in.

Dion said, "I will take the back and steer. Kim, why don't you sit at the helm and provide direction."

She said, "I will lead us on a successful journey downstream to the lake. Not slime nor rapids will splash in our way."

To which Dion replied, "A little dramatic, but I like it." Kim turned around and smiled back at him.

The currents were stronger than expected. The ride was beyond thrilling as everyone bounced in and out of their seats. Unadulterated fear began to set in as the gang questioned their very survival after facing multiple treacherous rapids in succession. Finally, at the brink of exhaustion, they came to a quiet part of the river. The shadow from the shoreline trees into the lake made it appear a beautiful emerald green.

It was a welcoming sight indeed after what they had just been through. However, it turned out to be the calm before the storm. Soon, the raft was swept downstream into a violent raging river that seemed to have no mercy on the flimsy inflatable craft. Dion tried his best to steer to the center of the river and maintain control over its trajectory but to no avail. The craft was yielding to the power of rapids.

He yelled, "Brace yourselves, we are at the mercy of the river."

Just then, Kim screamed, "There is a huge rock straight ahead!"

In that instant, a thought flashed into Nate's head: *I don't recall seeing that rock on our way up the river.*

There was no time to react. Before they knew it, they ran straight into the rock at full speed. As the water split around the rock to both sides, the raft shot straight up into the air like a snowboarder doing tricks in a halfpipe. The yielding craft went completely airborne as Kim yelled, "Everyone, hang on!"

Then, the raft came crashing back down onto the water with a hard splash on the opposite side of the boulder. Dion looked around. Someone was missing. Anthony had been thrown out of the boat!

Dion turned around and saw his friend clinging to the large rock they had just flown over. There was no way they could go back for him. The raging river's currents remained in command of the feather-light inflatable as it lunged forward with the rolling green abyss.

The gang was wondering what fate had in store for them.

Fortunately, just downstream, around a bend, the river widened. The rapids subsided, and Dion was able to guide the craft toward the shore. Kim barked out directions to avoid hitting large branches floating in the water that might damage their inflatable raft. "Steer left, and now right."

As soon as they reached the river's edge, the gang jumped out and began running back upstream toward Anthony.

"We must hurry," exclaimed Lucia. "I can't imagine Anthony will be able to hold on for long."

As they approached the rock, they could see he was now up on top of it. Somehow, he had managed to climb up that slimy rock that was as slippery as an ice glacier. No one was sure exactly how he did it.

Lucia called to Anthony, "Are you OK?"

Anthony replied, "I am looking good, sitting on this rock in the middle of the raging rapids of a slimy green river."

"You're amazing," said Lucia, out of breath.

Chelsea's eyes darted around before she remarked, "I don't see any way we can rescue him,"

The violet stream of green-white water was rushing around both sides of the huge rock. It was a treacherous situation by any measure.

As the group contemplated what to do, Anthony felt something underneath him. He yelled, "This rock is moving!"

The gang was thinking the worst, figuring the strong currents had dislodged it, and it was going to roll downstream and take Anthony with it.

Much to their surprise, it appeared to be moving sideways. Then, out of the water to one side, the head of a giant turtle appeared. Chelsea exclaimed, "This was not a rock at all—it is the shell of a giant turtle!"

The reptile slowly crawled to the shore right through the strong current as Anthony sat on its back, urging it to move toward the shore. The rest of the gang cheered him on, "Let's go, turtle!" as it brought him safely back to his friends.

"Now that is one big pappy snappy," Anthony chuckled. "I'm much obliged for the ride."

The gang decided to end their day on this note, unwilling to dive into another adventure.

* * *

For the rest of the week, they couldn't stop talking about the green, slimy lake and what might happen in their next adventure. While it had been quite frightening for a little while, they were all looking forward to jumping back into their virtual world the first chance they got and decided to meet in Kim's basement over the weekend.

On another Saturday morning, with a bit of trepidation, they once again entered the world of *The Lost View.*

What they saw was menacing. They realized the prehistoric reptile creature was completely delirious from all the green stuff she'd been eating. She was an enormous monster by this time, several times the size from the previous encounter.

Kim said, "She looks like some sort of an amphibious dinosaur. The creature was jumping straight up out of the water and then falling to her side back into it, creating a huge splash with each acrobatic maneuver.

Poor Tug rocked back and forth at the mercy of every lunge of the massive beast. The lake, on the other hand, was clearing up.

Kim remarked, "The lake is almost back to its normal brown color. This lack of food was making the beast even more agitated. She was hungry for that green stuff, and there was not much left of it to be found.

The seahorses had all taken shelter again, huddled together under some trees near the lake shore. Finally, after swimming in circles around the lake's perimeter, the monster found the entrance to the lake from the Wandering River and headed upstream against the current in search of slime. By this time, she was so strong and enormous that there was no stopping her. She jumped in and out of the water like a salmon going upriver to spawn. The gang followed her progress as she ate all the green slime in sight.

Eventually, she made her way upriver to the waterfalls where the students had their class picture taken at the end of last school year. By this time, the gang decided the monster needed a name.

Chelsea suggested, "Why don't we call her Katie Komo."

Nate replied, "I like the name. How did you decide that she was female?"

"No way for us to tell, but she looks good in green."

"Fair enough," replied Nate.

Katie crawled out of the water. To everyone's surprise, she had short, extremely agile legs. Katie had incredible grace and uncharacteristic mobility on land as well as in the water. She easily navigated the terrain, alongside the falls, up to the top, where she re-entered the water to resume her slime-eating rampage. Soon enough Katie made her way to the bridge across the Wandering River that was flooded last year when the boys crossed during their summer mountain adventure.

In an eating frenzy, the massive beast jumped so far out of the water that she landed clear up on top of the bridge, shattering the guard railing as she lunged to free herself from the bridge. She was agitated to say the least. So much so that she became tangled in the substantial steel cable railing that lined both sides of the bridge. She attempted to spin around on the narrow bridge several times in desperation, but the more she struggled to free herself, the more entangled she became.

The Sharefield Gang decided it was time to return to Moon Glow Lake. There, they found the water to be crisp and clear. The seahorses were once again out on the lake, tied up to Tug. Tug himself was pristine, his chrome glistening in the sun. One would think he had just been recommissioned. The friends all cheered at the sight.

After all that excitement, they decided to end their session for the day.

8

DISCOVERY DAY

No one understood why the green slimy stuff appeared in the first place, or where it came from, but it certainly gave the Sharefield Gang a new experience of unbridled excitement.

The following day, the friends decided to meet in Sharefield Park to consider what kind of adventure to set up next in their virtual world. It was a pity they still could not conduct their seahorse races because of all the unforeseen chaos in the virtual reality.

They stopped to get ice cream on their way to the park on Sunday afternoon. There, they ran into Brandon and Phillip.

The boys again thanked them for their support during last summer's mountain adventure. Then, they told the older boys about the world of *The Lost View*. Phillip was particularly fascinated, given his interest in computer technology. He suggested the gang decide on an event and then detail it among themselves before entering it into the artificial intelligence system through a voice description.

He said, "If you're specific enough with your description, your experience should be more accurate."

The friends thanked Phillip for his advice, and after considerable back-and-forth in the park, Dion suggested they go ahead with their seahorse races on the lake.

He remarked, "We could set up buoys to form an oval track and race our trusty seahorses around them."

"That sounds like it would be competitive," said Kim. "The oval track would give us lots of opportunity to jockey for position."

Dion replied, "I am looking forward to racing with you side by side on our gallant seahorses."

Chelsea interjected, "We could give prizes to the winner!"

"What kind of prizes?" Nate raised his brow.

Chelsea answered, "Well, you know, virtual prizes that have virtual value in our virtual world."

Everyone laughed. Filled with energy, they all agreed that the seahorse races would offer them mind-blowing fun, so the gang decided to go off and think about exactly how to orchestrate the race activity and what prizes might be awarded.

In their real world, the friends were looking forward to a school-sponsored Discovery Day the following week. There were lots of activities scheduled for learning outside of the classroom. The gang was particularly interested in a boat race that was to take place in a flowing water trough set up on the school grounds. They were drawn to this activity because so much of their virtual world involved water-related scenarios on Lake Moon Glow.

It was to be a timed event. The winner would be the fastest model boat to make it through the course from one end to the other. Each team of two students was given a kit of materials to construct their own watercraft. The kit contained cloth for a sail, several pieces of light wood, small bungee cords for propulsion, a couple of coins for weight distribution, glue, tape, and so forth. The student pairs could design their craft any way they chose. They could also name and paint their vessel in any color scheme that suited them. Nate loved watercraft, so he was obviously looking forward to it the most.

The gang decided to break up into three teams so they could all enter the event. Dion asked Kim if they could work together, and she happily agreed. Nate and Chelsea decided to work as a team. Anthony and Lucia joined forces with the feeling that their skills and personalities complemented each other so well that they should most certainly have an advantage over the others. Anthony exclaimed "Ships Ahoy!"

To which Lucia said, "That is my boy," as they both laughed.

The students received their materials kit on Monday afternoon, and they all began planning their racing vessel that very evening.

Kim and Dion met at Kim's house and laid out all the parts of the kit on a table. After some discussion, Dion said, "A catamaran with a sail would be fast because the narrow double halls will have minimum contact with the water surface, creating less drag."

This sounded good to Kim, but she had a couple concerns.

"You have a wonderful idea, Dion, but it will depend upon the wind the day of the race, no? We don't know how strong it'll be that day and if it will blow in the right direction. Have you thought about how it will steer since the course is not in a straight line?"

Dion agreed, "You are so right Kim, these are indeed valid concerns. I think the boat will make its way through the course without a steering mechanism because there will be a constant flow of water through the trough that will guide it along. The boat should act just like our virtual green watercraft," he explained, "following the current through the course around any bends or obstacles in front of it."

Kim said, "Well, you were trying to steer the raft in our green water adventure, so if you think the boat will steer itself, I agree with your assessment."

She paused for a moment before continuing. "But the wind is another consideration. What if it is blowing in the wrong direction to propel the boat forward? Since we can't steer, we can't tack upwind, and even if we could, it would be very slow."

"Good point," frowned Dion. "We need an alternate plan. If the wind is blowing strong, we can mount a premade sail atop our boat the morning of the race. If not, we need another way to propel it forward. Maybe we could make a paddle wheel that would fit between the catamaran's two hulls and drive it with the bungee cords supplied to us in the kit. We can wind up the cords, so they turn the paddle wheel as they unwind in the water."

Kim agreed, "This is a very versatile solution. If we have only a light breeze, maybe we can use both the sail and the paddle wheel together."

Dion replied, "That sounds fantastic!"

Nate and Chelsea were also considering how to construct their entry into the race. They were both impressed with Tug, their favorite virtual watercraft. He had shown his stripes in the tug-of-war match against Deep Dungeon.

"How can we construct a seaworthy craft like our tugboat?" asked Chelsea.

Nate replied, "Well, that should be possible with the materials we have in our kit. We can form the hull with the larger piece of balsa wood and carve a propeller from a couple of the smaller pieces to make one that looks just like Tug's. I got a good look at it when we were repairing him after the vicious tug of war."

Chelsea agreed. "Yes, if we run a couple bungee cords from the front to the back of the boat and attach them to the propeller, we can wind them up and they will spin the prop to victory."

"Bungee cords from forward to aft, I like it," nodded Nate with appreciation.

The dreaming team of Lucia and Anthony wanted to push the design envelope with something very different.

Lucia said, "Let's think of this at the most fundamental level. We want to go from the start to the finish line in the least amount of time. We have this kit full of stuff to help us to achieve that."

Anthony laughed and said, "That is fundamental, all right. So how do we build our boat? Sometimes you are difficult to understand."

Lucia, smiling, imagined herself as a particle traveling through the water from one end of the trough to the other. The force of the water against her was strong. It was much stronger than the force she normally felt in the air.

"That water is going to slow us down," she grimaced.

Anthony nodded. "Yes, boats don't travel as fast as planes. Water density is much greater than that of the air."

"Then maybe we should not build a boat," Lucia suggested.

Anthony looked at her funny.

Lucia explained, "Remember how Deep Dungeon took off and flew across the water when the rope broke in the tug-of-war competition with our beloved Tug? Maybe we should catapult our boat across the water toward the finish line."

Anthony said, "That's an interesting idea, but I have no idea how we can pull that off. We can't just slingshot our boat from one end to the other."

Lucia thought for a moment and then said, "Why not? We have bungee cords in our package to make a slingshot, just as you suggest."

"The rules stipulate that we must start at the starting line, which is in the water," Anthony countered.

Lucia replied, "Deep Dungeon started in the water, so why can't we launch our craft from the starting line and go air-borne over the trough to the finish line. There is not a water vessel on the planet that could do it any faster."

Anthony was skeptical but said, "OK, let's give our flying boat idea a shot. I like the way you think outside the trough."

"Since it is traveling through the air, we should design it more like a soaring rocket than a floating boat," Lucia suggested.

The pair set about making a rocket-like craft with a boat hull carved on the underside. They incorporated a slot across the back to hold the bungee cord they planned to attach across the trough and secure to its sides with a dowel rod. The rod would pass underneath the trough from one side to the other.

All three teams rushed to prepare their crafts for the big Discovery Day event. Kim told Dion, "We should paint our catamaran to look like a tiger with gold and black stripes."

"I like the way you're thinking," said Dion. "Since the fastest cat in the world is the cheetah, why don't we go with a gold base color combined with black spots and white highlights."

"That's perfect," said Kim. "Now we need a name. Our cat can stand up to any other vessel on the waterway."

After some research, the two of them settled on *Jabari*, which is fearless in Swahili.

Kim suggested, "Let's put 80CAT on the sail in recognition of the cheetah's incredible top speed of eighty miles an hour."

"Oh yeah," said Dion, "I can hear the name *Jabari* on the winner's podium already, as he gave his team partner a hug."

Nate and Chelsea called their vessel *Deep's Demise* in recognition of Tug's awesome performance in the virtual tug-of-war competition with Deep Dungeon. They painted their vessel white like Tug himself. If their beloved boat saw this tribute, he'd be over the moon!

Lucia asked Anthony, "What should we call our watercraft spaceship?"

Anthony thought momentarily, then replied, "How about *Flying Hull Y'all?*" Lucia said, "That name is as strange as the model itself. Let's paint it red on the tip, blue in the middle, and white on the back." Anthony said, "It'll look like a comet flying through the air."

"At the speed of lightning," added Lucia.

The big day had finally arrived. It was time to see whose entry was the fastest. Kim had a confident smile on her face, there was a strong wind blowing from the starting line directly toward the finish line.

"We're in luck," she said. "Let's mount both the sail and the paddle wheel so we'll have two methods of propulsion working together. This should really put us ahead of the others." Dion gave her a high five and mounted the sail on Jabari.

Nate and Chelsea's boat raced first, followed by several similar crafts. So far in the competition, *Deep's Demise* was holding on to first place. Then, it was Kim and Dion's turn to race *Jabari*. Thanks to the water flow in the trough, the boat did indeed steer itself just as Dion had predicted. It had an incredibly fast run. The bar had just been set higher for the other contestants as *Jabari* moved into first place.

A couple of other teams raced next but were no match for *Jabari*, which easily held on to first place. Then, a boat that looked remarkably like Kim and Dion's moved into the starting position. It was a catamaran with a sail, but the bungee propulsion system was set up much differently. It spun a propeller that was pointing straight down at the water.

"That's not going to help much," laughed Dion. "It's going to completely unspin the bungee cords long before the end of the course."

As this strange boat design left the starting line, the propeller spinning down at the water stopped halfway through the race since there was no water resistance to slow it down, just as Dion had predicted. However, something else happened: the fan blowing down at the water momentarily lifted the craft so that less of its twin halls were submerged. It accelerated quickly with less drag propelled by the strong tailwind blowing against its sail. This gave the craft an undisputed advantage, as it finished the race under sail as a more traditional seaworthy catamaran.

"Wow, that was impressive," said Kim.

"What just happened?" replied Dion.

When the time for the run was posted, it beat *Jabari* by a full two seconds, placing Kim and Dion in second place. Dion said to Kim in a consoling voice, "Second place to that ingenious design is not bad at all."

The final entry to complete the course was Lucia and Anthony's *Flying Hull Y'all*. As they set up the slingshot bungee and attached their craft, the other students looked on with limitless curiosity. The *Flying Hull Y'all* team tried to ignore their questions, they had a race to run. As the starting horn blew, Anthony pulled the craft back, extending the bungee cords while Lucia helped steady the flying craft in the water precisely at the starting line. Then Anthony and Lucia let go at the same time. Their boat immediately left the water and flew toward the finish line at an incredible speed. It was headed straight for the finish line banner. It tore through it, then continued forward for several more feet before stopping in the grass. It was pointing backwards and upside down.

The students cheered, but the judges did not know what to make of it. That vessel was by far the fastest craft, but it did not follow the water path through the trough. After some deliberation, the teachers judging the competition decided that *Flying Hull Y'all* should be disqualified because it did not negotiate the turns in the course that were intended to measure each of the crafts' maneuverability.

However, the judges gave Lucia and Anthony an award for being the most creative entry in the race. Kim and Dion were awarded second place behind the air lift-assisted catamaran. Nate and Chelsea also got an award; theirs was for the best-made, most aesthetically pleasing design. That award was warmly satisfying to Nate because he and Chelsea took a lot of pride in the meticulously detailed construction of the miniature Tug reproduction.

After the boat race competition, the friends proceeded to check out several of the other exhibits that were set up for Discovery Day. One of particular interest was a demonstration of water density. Lucia saw it first.

"Look," she pointed out. "Let's investigate the table over there with different glasses of water on it."

One glass had ice floating on top of the water, the second contained a ball that had sunk to the bottom, and the third had an identical ball floating on top of the water. Ms. Jenkins, the science teacher, was at the table explaining the difference to everyone stopping by.

She pointed to the first glass and said, "Everyone knows that ice floats, but do you know why? Ice is a few percent lighter than liquid water, so it sets on top of it. When ice forms, it expands, becoming less dense than liquid water. The ball in the middle glass is slightly heavier than normal drinking water, so it sinks to the bottom. The third glass has saltwater in it, like our oceans. The salt makes the water heavier, so the same ball is less dense than the salt water and floats on top of it."

"This is all very interesting. Why is it that the oceans are so salty in the first place?" asked Lucia.

"That's a very good question," said Ms. Jenkins. "Much of the salt comes from the rivers that flow into the sea. They pick up minerals and salt from the rock that they flow over. The salt ends up in the ocean. The rivers themselves get replenished with fresh rainwater and melting snow, so they are not as salty."

Then, remembering something from one of his classes, Dion asked, "Why is the Caribbean Sea so blue?"

"It has to do with how sunlight is scattered when it hits the water," Ms. Jenkins smiled. "Just as a prism shows all the colors in the rainbow coming from the sun, the water reflects the blue light that we see and absorbs the other colors."

"That's very cool," said Dion.

"And beautiful," added Kim.

"Isn't it?" Ms. Jenkins nodded.

The gang moved on to another display showing a miniature wave machine inside a clear plastic tank. The tank tilted back and forth as the water inside formed a wave moving from side to side. Chelsea liked that display. She said, "I would like to learn how to surf someday. "What causes waves along the shore of the oceans?" she asked.

Standing nearby, another teacher, Mr. Thomas, heard Chelsea's question and said, "What do *you* think causes the waves?"

Chelsea shrugged. "I really don't know."

Anthony replied, "I think it has something to do with the gravity on the moon."

"Not exactly," said Mr. Thomas, "but you're close. The moon's gravitational force pulls on the oceans as the Earth spins; this causes the water to move toward and away from the shores, creating high and low tides. So, the moon influences the oceans but does not actually cause the waves that rush to the shore."

"Well then," said Chelsea, "what *does* cause the waves?"

Mr. Thomas replied, "It's the wind. As the wind blows over the vast surface area of the seas, the sheer forces against the water cause the water to lift and move in waves toward the shore. It's like running your hand across your pillow; it makes a small wave in front of it. Of course, the wind is more widespread, but it can only move so much water at a time, depending on how strong it is. The frequency of waves crashing into the shore varies but is generally around five to eleven times every minute."

"If I ever have the chance to learn how to surf someday," said Chelsea. "I will be looking for those windy waves!"

The gang moved on to the next display. It showed two models of sea coral in an aquarium. The one on the left was beautifully colored and eye-catching. The one on the right was pure white. The sign above the display said that ocean warming was causing the coral to lose its color.

"This reminds me of the shipwreck in our theater production," observed Nate. "All the coral around the sunken ship was white. Jimmy must have known that warming seas were bleaching out the coral."

"It's such a shame," said Kim. "I think the colors in the coral are just beautiful."

There was one more display at Discovery Day that the gang wanted to see. It was a booth to teach students about microplastics in the seas and oceans. According to the display, very small plastic particles, which may be the size of the thickness of a human hair are contaminating the oceans. Many plastics from paint, cosmetics, and other human products can end up in the oceans. Fish eat these microplastics, and so do humans. The very small plastic particles in the oceans can last for hundreds of years before they decay, so the problem is bound to get worse as time goes on, according to the information on the display board. The group found this to be especially alarming.

"Who wants to be eating plastic?" said Lucia, looking aghast. "It doesn't sound like a good thing to me."

Anthony replied, his expression solemn, "Maybe that's why my knuckles crack sometimes. They are breaking up the plastic inside me."

As another teacher, Ms. Wang, walked by, she commented, "Mother Nature is resilient, and so are we. There are problems in the oceans and all around the world, but there are also smart people, just like you, who are already working on them."

Everyone in the gang agreed that Discovery Day held unexpected gems of knowledge. It was delightfully amusing and packed with diverse insights on the most basic of Earth's resources.

Dion said, "We learned so much about water. It's something we just take for granted every day. I see it differently now."

His friends murmured their agreement.

9

SEAHORSE UNDERWATER ADVENTURE

Inspired by all their newfound knowledge about water from Discovery Day, the gang agreed to meet again to plan for the virtual seahorse races on Lake Moon Glow. Walking around the park, they decided there would be three races, each consisting of two laps around the lake, with Tug positioned in the center to assist them. Like the Discovery Day race, Tug would sound his horn to start each race, and in case of a tie, they agreed to run the race again. With everything settled, there was no reason for further delay. The first race was scheduled for next Monday after school, and all the friends were thrilled!

They arrived at Kim's house on the scheduled afternoon and went straight to her basement for the session. They were once again surprised as they put on their glasses and looked out over Lake Moon Glow. Something was very strange. Tug was sitting in the middle of the lake by himself.

Chelsea voiced what they were all thinking at that moment, "Where are our seahorses?"

The gang scanned the entire lake and the adjoining shoreline. The seahorses were simply nowhere to be found.

"This is terribly disappointing, to say the least," muttered Dion.

He placed himself inside the virtual world to better search for the missing seahorses. As he investigated the tree-lined shore on the east end of the lake for any clues of the seahorses, he feared the worst. Then, from out of the thick brush between the trees, a magnificent monarch butterfly suddenly appeared. It bounced through the air with effortless freedom just in front of him.

Dion recalled, *This creature looks just like the butterfly that emerged from its chrysalis last year, from the caterpillar we found on our trip up Majestic Mountain last summer. I will never forget the day it took flight from its chrysalis. It hovered around me and then landed directly on my hand before flying away, not to be seen again. At the time, I thought it was an omen of some sort.*

Then he remembered Lucia telling the gang that those butterflies migrate thousands of miles to warmer climates for the winter months. The following generations return to the same general area where the offspring's ancestors left.

Dion marveled at nature's wonders just as he had the day Lucia first told him of the monarch's migration habits.

He thought, *Maybe this is a descendant of the special butterfly from last year that's now in our virtual world.*

Almost on cue, the butterfly fluttered next to him, landed on his hand only for a second, and then flew off. This action was eerily similar to the one from the year before. Back then, too, at Victor's house, the monarch butterfly gently touched his hand in the same way soon after it emerged from its chrysalis to first see the light of day.

Simultaneously, the spinning key appeared in the lower right-hand corner of his view.

Why is the key there? Dion wondered. *What is making it spin like that?*

He was perplexed. He didn't understand the significance of this and asked the others in the room if they saw the monarch or the spinning key. No one else reported seeing any such thing except Chelsea who happened to notice the spinning key. As he tracked the beautiful monarch butterfly, he could see it fly out over Lake Moon Glow, dip down toward the water and then rise again.

That's strange, it doesn't need to drink from that big lake. Dion had no explanation for the behavior.

The fluttering butterfly continued this for several minutes. As bizarre as this was, Dion had a feeling it was trying to tell him something, pointing down below the water's surface. He turned his attention to the lake before him as his eyes drifted under its surface to the bed of Lake Moon Glow. What he saw next absolutely astounded him. He could see under the water as clear as day!

It turned out the seahorses were interested in their own little adventure. They had been covered in slime and wanted to get cleaned up, and apparently, they longed for their natural habitat under the sea just off the coast of the Caribbean Islands.

Dion laughed, "Do we have sea home-sick seahorses?"

"What are you talking about?" asked Kim.

"Take a look for yourselves. Just look under the water," said Dion.

Perplexed, the gang focused their glasses where Dion requested. They could see what appeared to be a beautifully colored coral reef on the edge of an island.

It was indeed the Caribbean Sea. There, under the water, were the six seahorses chasing each other around with lightning speed and breathtaking agility. In their view was an abundance of beautifully colored tropical fish of varied species.

Lucia noticed, "The fish are all avoiding the seahorses."

As the gang looked on, they could tell that the seahorses were pilfering food from the fish.

"I don't believe what I am seeing," marveled Anthony. "Our seahorses are pirates in the Caribbean of Moon Glow Lake!"

"Yes, that appears so," said Nate.

"Well," Kim sighed, "we cannot race today. There are pirates at large in the sea under Lake Moon Glow. Shame on them. Maybe we'll have better luck tomorrow. I suggest we leave the seahorses to their mischief and come back later. Maybe by then, they will be ready for our racing event."

Anthony said, "I hope the pirates can race as fast as they are running from that mad grouper chasing after them."

Lucia shook her head. "You can't blame him. Look at what Clyde Sail has in his mouth!"

It was a small fish, evidently the grouper's dinner. Just then, the arm of an octopus reached out from behind a rock and snagged the fish right out of Clyde Sail's mouth with its tentacles. In one smooth motion, it flicked the fish backward behind the startled seahorse and directly into the mouth of the hungry grouper.

Nate said, "I knew my Clyde Sail was a little feisty, but I didn't realize that seahorses had such a devilish streak."

"They all appear to be that way," commented Dion. "We'll have to be on guard during our races tomorrow with this pirate breed of seahorses carrying us around."

"That's for sure," agreed Kim. "I don't fancy getting caught up in these dastardly delinquent deeds, and look over there, Ski Dattle is doing *sea salty seahorse somersaults* in the water. You know, I think he's trying to impress Water Chestnut. She's blushing. What a little firecracker! Water Chestnut may be a good match for him. I cannot wait to see if the sparks fly between them or fizzle out."

"These seahorses are all trying to outdo one another," giggled Lucia. "Look, Poky Hokey Dokey is just standing there daring the others to hit him with a starfish. He is so fast; he can dodge them every single time."

"Our races on these devilish sea creatures are going to be contentious," observed Dion.

With that, the gang decided to sign off their world in *The Lost View* and meet the following day, hoping the seahorses would be finished 'horsing' around in their undersea adventure and ready for some serious racing.

On the way home, Dion stopped at one of the busier streets in town, like he always does on his way home from Kim's, and pushed the crosswalk button. As the *Walk* sign lit up, he began crossing the street when he happened to catch sight of a utility van out of the corner of his eye. It was a cosmetics delivery truck decorated with a monarch butterfly logo.

For a brief second, he froze. *What a coincidence*, he thought, and moved on.

At that very instant, out of nowhere, a car came speeding from the other direction through the light into the intersection before him. Horror-struck, Dion realized if he had stepped onto the street when the crosswalk sign blinked *WALK*, he most assuredly would have been hit.

Did the monarch butterfly on the side of that van just save his life?

* * *

The following afternoon, the Sharefield Gang met again in Kim's basement, and Dion explained what had happened to him on his walk home the previous day.

He whispered, "I don't know how, and I may sound a little crazy to you, but I'm convinced this was not some random event."

Instead of mocking him, his friends gaped at him.

Chelsea responded, "You know, I remember seeing the spinning key about the time Dion saw the monarch yesterday. This is a very strange coincidence. Why did the spinning key appear? I bet there's a connection here."

Nate agreed. "It's strange, indeed, Dion. I remember when the real monarch butterfly landed on your hand last summer. How often does a butterfly actually land on someone's hand?"

IO

SEAHORSE RACE DAY

As the Sharefield Gang put on their glasses to enter the world of *The Lost View* once again, they found all the seahorses tied up to Tug, just like they had expected to see the day before.

"OK," said Dion, "it looks like it's finally race day."

They each called their seahorse to the shore and saddled up. They all looked a bit skittish and overtly energetic after their underwater adventure. Their riders commanded a couple of practice laps on their mounts, slow at first and then a bit quicker, but saving the all-out sprints for the race. After a few warm-up laps, everyone was ready to go.

All six seahorses lined up at the starting line, and Tug blew his horn. They were off and gliding across the lake!

Lucia on Water Chestnut took an early lead down the straightaway and around the first curve. Then Kim on Aquastrian passed her on the back straightaway. Anthony felt, early on, that Poky was just holding back, waiting for the right moment. He was running in fifth place but was not worried because Poky was hardly putting forth any effort.

Clyde Sail passed Aquastrian at the start of the second lap, and then Sea Biscotti retook the lead on the back straightaway. There was only half of a lap to go when Poky suddenly came to life. He took off through the water like the rocket boat Anthony and Lucia had built for the school Discovery Day. Anthony passed his friends one by one, then splashed by Chelsea on Sea Biscotti to stop right at the finish line.

Everyone congratulated Anthony for his star performance.

He humbly replied, "It was all Poky. All I did was hold onto her fins and give her a kick in the shins."

Lucia questioned; her eyebrows raised. "Just where are the shins on a seahorse?"

Anthony shrugged. "Whatever, we won."

By this time, it was getting late, and the seahorse manure was getting thicker. The creatures and their riders were exhausted, so the gang decided to call it a day and head home.

On the way out the door from Kim's house, Nate remarked, "I have to admit I'm absolutely astounded and truly overwhelmingly impressed with the power of our virtual world."

Hearing Nate's comment, Chelsea responded, "It *is* clearly out of this world as we know it."

The gang was anxious to continue their racing, but they all needed to attend to other things in the real world. So, they decided to meet again after school in the middle of the following week for the second race.

Wednesday of the next week rolled around in a flash, and it was racing day once again.

As everyone put on their glasses that day in the basement, the seahorses seemed to know what was coming and were ready to go.

The gang all thought Anthony and Poky were favorites to win the race again, but the others were all determined to give this two-lap sprint their absolute best effort.

As Tug's horn sounded, the seahorses all took off in a flash, carrying their overzealous riders on their backs. Yelling and cheering down the first straightaway, they all tapped their seahorse with their legs, encouraging them to kick some splash. Maybe somehow, this way, they'd find the shins!

This time, it was Dion and Ski Dattle all the way. Chelsea riding Sea Biscotti gave a good fight at the end to come in a close second. Nate riding Clyde Sail was third. Anthony on Poky came in dead last, way behind the rest of the field.

After the race, Anthony commented sadly, "There must be something wrong with poor Poky. Perhaps she was sick; she seemed to have no energy at all."

As the seahorses all went to the food trough, Poky moved at the speed of her name and got there last. As she settled down, she started gobbling up the feed in sheer desperation.

Anthony noted, "It appears she's been starving for days."

As it turned out, that was exactly what had happened. She hadn't had much to eat at all since the last race. The other rather divisive seahorses had worked together to keep her away from the food trough after she won the first race so handily.

Once Anthony figured out what had caused him to lose the second race, he thought it best to sit the next one out. This would give poor Poky Hokey Dokey a chance to rest up and recover from near starvation.

He told the others, "I'll be happy to be the announcer and call the race for the rest of you."

The others agreed it was a good plan.

Kim made it a point to put on her glasses to check on the seahorses each day after that second race until the weekend when the third was planned. She wanted to make sure that all the racing seahorses got sufficient nourishment.

The following Saturday, everyone was prepared for the third and final race. The Sharefield Gang was psyched up!

Dion said, "I'll glide Ski Dattle to victory for the Moon Glow Crown."

The others all felt the same about their chances of winning the 'big one.'

As they put on their glasses and mounted their seahorses, Anthony and Poky Hokey Dokey moved to the edge of the lake where Anthony would have a good vantage point of everything happening. He saw the others warming up their seahorses, preparing for the grand finale. All the seahorses sensed the excitement of the big event and were behaving somewhat out of control. They lined up at the starting point as Anthony took over the commentary.

"We have perfect conditions out on Lake Moon Glow today. It should be a very exciting race indeed. But first, a word from our sponsor. Sandy's Seahorse Saddles are second to none. Sit your backside down in one and have some fun. Available in six shades for any seahorse of a different color. Now for the race, our contestants are all lined up and ready to start. We should have a soaking-fast one today. There is the starting horn from Tug, and they are off!

"It is Clyde Sail first out of the gate. Well, we don't actually have a gate, but you get it. Anyway, he is in the early lead, followed by Aquastrian to the outside. In the center, half of a seahorse's tailback is Water Chestnut as we head into the first turn. Now charging from the center of the splash on the backstretch is Ski Dattle. He is trying to make a move, but the wake from the pack is blocking him. He just doesn't have the wave. Clyde Sail is still in the lead but is being challenged by Sea Biscotti right alongside. "Oh, let me tell you that they are fast, really fast. The water is cold in Lake Moon Glow, but the pace is steaming hot here at the halfway point. In fact, I see steam rise from the water surface, or maybe it's mist from seahorse full-bodied dynamic tail propulsion, I can't tell at this point.

"Now it's Water Chestnut that surges ahead and takes the lead around the far turn of the second lap. It is Water Chestnut battling it out for the first place with both Sea Biscotti and Clyde Sail. Wait a couple splashes, now it is Aquastrian making a move to challenge from the outside, throwing water behind her into Ski Dattle's face. Well, eat my bubbles, I have never seen anything like this. Look, Ski Dattle is having nothing of that, as he charges to the inside and overtakes Aquastrian to challenge the three leaders, Clyde Sail, Water Chestnut, and Sea Biscotti."

Having a magnificent time as the event's commentator, Anthony continued his lighthearted delivery. Then things got serious, "Oh no, something just went drastically wrong for Ski Dattle. Dion is leaning way over to one side, almost falling off his seaworthy seahorse. He is totally out of control as Ski Dattle's tail flips to the side to hold himself upright. He is dropping off the pack. Meanwhile, Water Chestnut and Sea Biscotti are fighting it out wave to wave as Clyde Sail makes a move. It is down to the wire—if we had one. All three seahorses are forming a perfect line. It is a photo finish, just too darn close for me to call. What an exciting event! Folks, we have never witnessed such an event in the history of Moon Glow seahorse racing. This is one for the record books, my friends."

Immediately after the race, everyone turned their attention to Dion and Ski Dattle. What could have possibly happened in that race to cause Dion to lose complete control over his seahorse and end up so far behind the pack in last place, especially after winning the race before? Ski Dattle was clearly the strong favorite going into this derby.

Fortunately, Dion was not hurt, and neither was Ski Dattle. However, it appeared that Ski Dattle's saddle, a custom Sandy Seahorse model, needed repair. The strap around the mighty seahorse to hold the saddle in place had snapped completely in two. No wonder Dion lost control! There was no way to hold tension on the reigns with the loose saddle. A custom-made Sandy Seahorse saddle would not break on its own. No way. It was top quality. The gang suspected the other seahorses were once again up to foul play.

Kim said, "These seahorses cannot be trusted."

Nobody disagreed.

Anthony said, "I suspect the other seahorses rigged the last two races after I won the first one, fair and square and wet all over."

The gang decided to nullify the race winners and hold off giving any awards to the participants.

Not only was the behavior of the seahorses quite strange, but the sudden appearance of the spinning key in the screen's lower right-hand corner had everyone baffled yet again.

They all saw it flicker onto their screens just as Dion lost control of Ski Dattle.

There was no explanation as to why it was there.

Kim, who had taken a picture of the key one evening after school and included it in her upload to the virtual reality system for good luck, was now as perplexed as the rest of the gang.

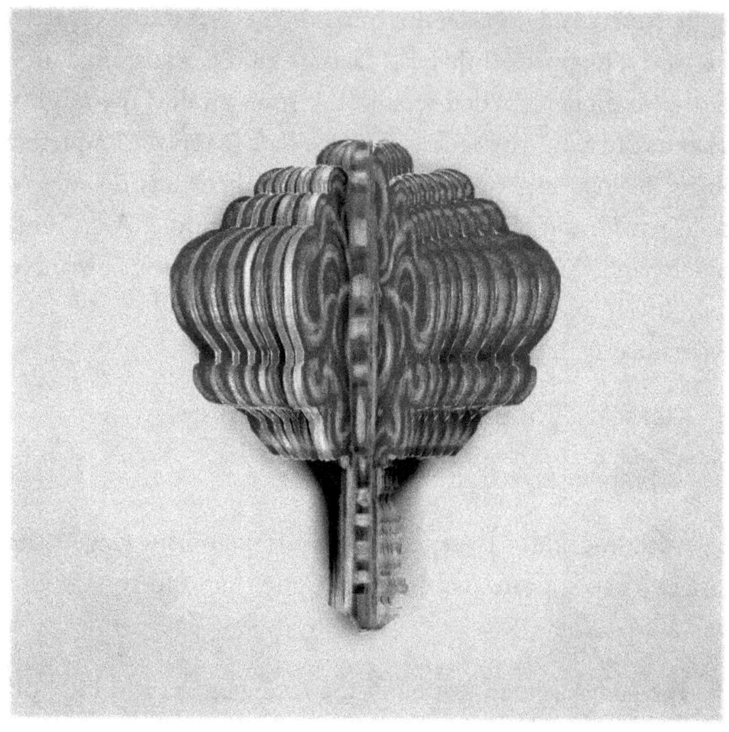

"How and why is this key showing up seemingly randomly?" she asked no one in particular.

Chelsea replied, "There must be a reason for it, right? We have to unwind this mind-spinning mystery."

And while nobody disagreed, they all silently wondered, *How?*

11

TRIP TO DIYTON

Fortunately, Dion was not hurt during the last race, and neither was his seahorse. However, Ski Dattle's saddle was in definite need of repair.

Dion knew that to fix it, he would need a new leather strap. There were no spare parts on Tug. Nate had entered the Sharefield Hardware store into the virtual reality system as part of their initial data-gathering exercise.

He waved his hand before his glasses and said, "Take me to the Sharefield Hardware Store."

In a flash, Nate walked into the store, looking for a leather strap to help his friend. Unfortunately, there was nothing there that could be used to fix Ski Dattle's saddle. It was a small store with limited supplies. The Sharefield store did not carry Sandy Seahorse supplies.

The closest town was Diyton, about ten miles to the north. The gang decided to end their virtual reality session at this point and then try to figure out how to get Dion up and riding again in *The Lost View* with the rest of them.

Nate's family planned to go to Diyton for some home repair supplies unavailable in Sharefield over the next week. They made the short trip to Diyton often since they were doing some remodeling at their residence.

Nate told the gang, "I can go along with my parents and collect some video of a couple of the stores in Diyton while I am there. Then we can input that data into the world of *The Lost View* so that Dion can shop there for the part he needs to repair his saddle."

As planned, Nate got plenty of videos around Diyton, including the hardware store and one of its employees. He remarked to his parents that the store had a much more extensive inventory than Sharefield. Nate shared the data with the rest of the gang the following weekend and uploaded the videos into the virtual reality system. The friends assumed the artificial intelligence program would allow Dion to be present in Diyton and acquire the leather strap.

Everyone signed on after inputting the Diyton image data. Unfortunately, there was no way to get to Diyton. Dion and the gang moved around from place to place throughout Sharefield, but they could not find a way to Diyton.

This puzzled them. Dion said, "I can create a map here in our virtual world, including Diyton. Why can't I find a way to get there?"

Lucia asked, "Nate, did you collect a video of the trip from Sharefield to Diyton?"

"Well, no," hesitated Nate. "It didn't even occur to me."

"That might be the problem," nodded Chelsea.

"We better hurry, then. It will surely be a long ten-mile walk if we can't figure something out soon," said Dion. It was starting to turn dark in their virtual world.

Dion was disappointed. He looked up at the moon shining down on the lake and said, "I wish I could walk like I was on the moon where gravity is only one-sixth that of earth." He had inadvertently waved his hand over the front of his glasses as he pointed toward the moon.

Instantly, there appeared some strange-looking machine beside him. The whole gang peered at it.

Dion said, "What in our artificial world is this contraption?" He referred to it as a contraption because he had no idea what it was or what it was for. It looked like a small trampoline on top of some flying craft.

Lucia suggested, "Dion, you should jump on it and see what happens."

Without thinking much about it, Dion stood on top of the contraption. The trampoline was only a couple of feet in diameter. He began to bounce up and down slowly. He said,

"This is the smallest trampoline I have ever encountered. I am afraid to bounce very high or I might miss it altogether when I come down. There is no telling what I would injure if that happened."

As he bounced softly, he said, "Okay, I am getting the hang of this. I am walking on the moon but can't go anywhere."

He stepped back off the trampoline and asked the rest of the gang, "What do you think I should do?"

Chelsea said, "Let me try." She jumped on and immediately started bouncing up as high as she could.

"Watch out!" warned Lucia.

Just as she screamed at Chelsea, she got off-center and was about to come crashing down off the extreme edge of the trampoline surface. To everyone's surprise, the trampoline shifted directly under her feet. She made another softer bounce and then stopped. Everyone was amazed. "Well, that was a leap of faith," said Anthony.

Dion said, "We have to investigate this further."

Looking closer, he could see that underneath the trampoline, there were propellers that could potentially spin and lift the trampoline off the ground.

"The contraption underneath the trampoline resembles a drone!" Lucia exclaimed. "It rose just off the ground and followed Chelsea and then landed so she would not miss it on her next bounce."

Dion said, "Very interesting. I wonder if it does that every time."

Nate replied, "Well, if it does, you have your moonwalker."

Dion nodded. "That would be very cool indeed. The only way to find out is to try it."

"How can we do that safely?" asked Kim.

Dion suggested that Nate and Anthony stand on one side of the contraption. He said, "I will jump a few times and then jump off to the side between the two of you so that we can see if the contraption moves. You can support me as I come down if it does not."

Anthony agreed. "That sounds like a good plan. The jury is still out on this Jumping Gyro."

Kim interjected, "Please be careful; you do not want to injure your virtual self or anything else."

So, the boys set up to perform the stunt. The propeller blades on the contraption were not moving as Dion began to jump up and down. After several jumps, he told the others, "Here I go, get ready to catch me."

This time, as he left the trampoline surface, the props instantly began to turn at an incredible speed. The contraption lifted just off the ground, darted to a position directly under Dion, and then set itself back down on stable Earth to support Dion's weight upon impact. Nate and Anthony had to jump out of the way to avoid being run over by the contraption, which appeared to have a mind of its own. Sure enough, Dion came down right in the middle of the trampoline as Nate and Anthony, with their arms outstretched to catch Dion, looked on in amazement. "I can hardly believe what we just witnessed," said Kim.

Dion said, "This time, I will jump farther off-center and see if the drone follows me."

Again, as soon as he jumped off the trampoline at an angle that would propel him forward, the drone-like contraption immediately responded and centered itself directly under where he was to land. Dion began to bounce around the area as the trampoline contraption followed his every bounce then stabilized itself on the ground with ultimate precision each time before he landed.

"This is so incredible!" Dion exclaimed. "I have a moon-walking machine. I can moonwalk over to Diyton on this unbelievable bouncing bundle of innovation in record time."

Kim suggested, "Perhaps you can make the trip on our next virtual reality session. Let's take some test drives today and fool around on this thing. It looks like a blast."

Dion smiled. "It is a blast-off for sure. It never misses positioning itself underneath me no matter how I jump."

"Let me give it a try," said Kim. She jumped up on the contraption and began bouncing around the shoreline of Lake Moon Glow like a pro. She was covering eight feet in every jump. It gave her a feeling of weightless jubilation, just like walking on the moon. Everyone wanted to try it next. They all took turns bouncing around the perimeter of the lake. The seahorses looked slightly jealous of the gang's ability to get around without them, while Tug appeared to be smiling at the spectacle.

The revolutionary moonwalking machine was a surprising and amusing experience for everyone who tried it. No matter how high one jumped, the contraption never seemed to miss. The gang came to trust the machine that could take off, move to where they would fall, land, and secure itself before the next bounce.

Anthony said, "Enough of this elation over levitation. We need to get back to reality."

To which Chelsea replied, "Our moonwalker needs a name."

Everyone thought about it momentarily, then threw out a couple of suggestions.

Finally, Anthony said, "Why don't we call it The Jumping Gyro? That is what I thought of it the first time I saw it move with Dion's bounce."

Kim said, "The way it jerks from place to place as you jump on it is astonishing." So, from then on, it became known as The Jerky Jumping Gyro, or the JJG for short.

The gang agreed to meet again the next day for Dion's trip to Diyton. He would make the journey by himself. The JJG was one-person transportation. The rest of the group, who would be staying behind, planned a virtual reality party.

Kim said, "Let's make it a Caribbean affair along the shore of Lake Moon Glow."

After everyone finished their schoolwork the following day, they met again in Kim's basement for their next adventure in *The Lost View*. After putting on their glasses, they waved goodbye to Dion as he took off on the ten-mile journey to Diyton on the JJG. It was easy going for him the first mile. He gained confidence in the craft and started jumping even higher than his test runs the day before. He noticed a green light on the side of the craft that would light up every time his feet left the trampoline surface.

After jumping as high as he possibly could, he noticed the light on the side of the JJG turned yellow as his feet lifted off the trampoline. He quickly realized that this light was an indicator of the JJG's capability. He pushed the JJG to its limits, covering up to ten feet of distance with every bounce. He was having a blast-off, so to speak. He knew he was safe if the indicator light remained green or yellow.

Meanwhile, the rest of the gang was setting up their virtual party. They structured it to be very realistic, just like the theater performance they had all experienced earlier in the year. They started doing some of the same dance routines and singing the songs they all knew so well from the performance.

Dion was making good progress until he encountered some steep hills in the second half of his journey. The JJG would steady itself on the hills after each jump, but it was setting at an angle, forcing Dion to make shorter advances up the hills and huge leaps down. The JJG could hardly keep up on the downhill slopes. On one particularly steep hill, Dion noticed the craft lit up red as his feet left the trampoline. He looked down below him and saw his craft was behind him and would not catch up before he landed. He hit the ground and tumbled down the hill with the JJG chasing him. They both stopped at the bottom of the hill in a tall grassy area. Dion was a little shaken. He stood up slowly and walked around a little. He thought, *None of my imaginary parts appear to be virtually broken. I believe I am good to go.*

He jumped back on the JJG. He was eager to continue his journey and didn't want to waste any time. However, he realized he had better take it easy, especially on the downhill slopes, if he wanted to arrive in Diyton in one piece.

Shortly after, he found himself at the entrance to the hardware store. The journey took less than an hour. He realized a well-trained marathon runner would take about the same time to cover that cross-country distance. *JJG and I are Olympic runner fast, huh,* he thought.

Once he arrived at the hardware store, he ran into one of the associates. "Hello, I am George, how can I help you?"

Dion replied, "I need a leather strap for a custom Sandy Saddle."

"I have just the strap for you," smiled George. He entered the back room and returned with a thick, strong leather piece.

Dion thanked him, saying, "This is just what I need to get back in the saddle of Ski Dattle."

He took it easy on the trip back to Sharefield, not wanting to fall again. The rest of the gang was beginning to wonder what was taking him so long. As Dion returned to town, he knew the neighborhood he was traveling through quite well. He had lived in Sharefield all his life.

Between bounces, he did a double take and noticed that one of the houses on the street was missing. There was an empty lot where the house once stood.

That's strange, he thought.

He didn't know the occupants personally but had seen the family from time to time. There was no doubt in his mind that a couple of young children lived there with their parents. At about the same time, the spinning key mysteriously appeared again in the lower right of his field of view. Dion was quite confused. He peered closely at it to see if it was the same key as the one in their theater production. It was the same shape Chelsea and the others had seen before. However, since it was spinning, he could not make out enough detail to know that it was exactly the same key.

He proceeded on his journey home to join his friends just finishing their Caribbean party. They were all happy to see him return home safely.

Dion held his leather strap and proclaimed, "The JJG is a remarkable land-worthy craft. Transportation has never been so amusing and dependable. It was truly like walking on the moon."

Kim replied, "We are all very happy to see your virtual self home safely and in the comfort of your friends."

Dion mentioned, "I saw something strange on the way back from Diyton. There was a missing house on Mulberry Street as the spinning key appeared in the lower left-hand corner of my view."

Everyone was as puzzled as he was; there was simply no explanation. Despite the mystery, the gang was elated with a successful virtual session as they signed off and headed home for dinner with their families.

The gang decided to get back together for their next session on the weekend. Dion was eager to fix Ski Dattle's saddle and start riding again. After everyone put on their glasses to continue the world of *The Lost View*, Dion worked on the saddle while the rest of the gang mounted their untrusty sea creatures and began riding around the lake. As Dion buckled the new strap in place after attaching it to his saddle, he noticed a number burnt into the back of the leather strap. He did not think much of it then, dismissing it as a probable serial number of the part used for manufacturing and inventory purposes. He got Ski Dattle back together in no time, then hopped on.

"It sure feels good to be back in the saddle, on my seahorse, riding with the rest of you," he smiled.

It was clear that Ski Dattle was enjoying it as much as he was. Not much was going on at Lake Moon Glow, so the gang cut their virtual reality session short and moved on to their responsibilities for the day.

That night, Dion tossed and turned in his bed, unable to stop thinking about the missing house on Mulberry Street.

The more he dwelled on it, the more he felt there must be some significance—especially since the spinning key appeared mysteriously, even though he had no idea what that meant. Then he thought about the number on the leather strap. *It was not a particularly unusual number, but I did not expect the strap to have a number burned into it. I wonder if there is something special about it,* he thought.

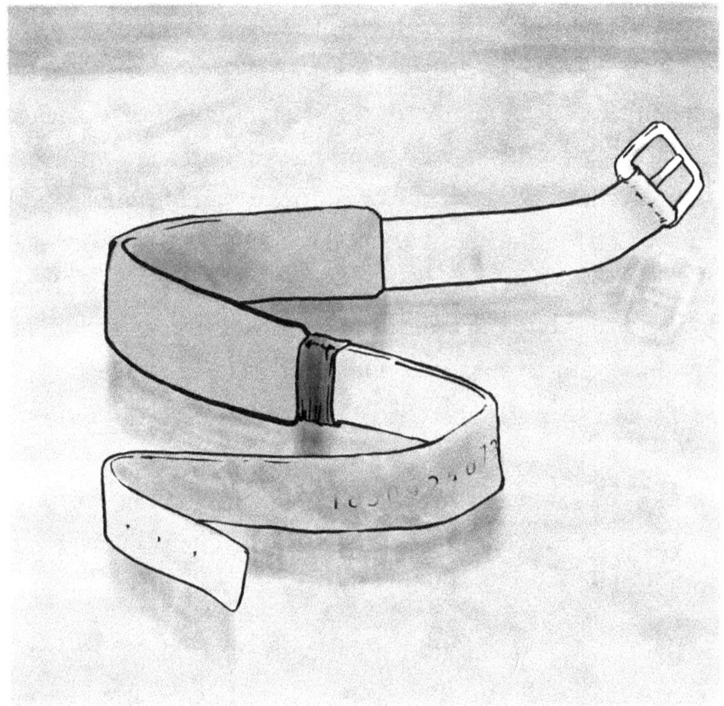

Then he suddenly realized it was a ten-digit number and remembered vividly seeing it. *Ten digits,* he thought. *Could it possibly be a phone number? It was unlikely, but then again, maybe it could be.*

His curiosity got the best of him, and he jumped out of bed and dialed the number from the leather strap. The phone rang, but no one answered. His curiosity had been satisfied. He thought no more of it and went off to sleep.

The next morning, his father commented that he had just watched the news.

"A house on Mulberry Street burned to the ground last night," he said. "The firefighters arrived on the scene, but the town water pressure had been significantly reduced due to some algae contamination in the reserve supply that clogged up the system. Only a fraction of the water pressure was available to them. There were no injuries," he continued. "The family, along with their two small children, escaped the blaze just in time. The family had gone to bed early. Evidently, a mysterious phone call around 11 p.m. woke them up and allowed them to escape. That phone call saved their lives."

What...?

Dion just stared at his dad with a blank look on his face. He didn't know what to say. That was when he placed the call from his bedroom last night, didn't he?

That afternoon, he told his friends what had happened. Everyone got chills up their spines. Then Lucia started to put some of the pieces together.

"Wait a minute," she said. "The spinning key appeared in the lower right hand of our view when you saw the missing house, right?"

Dion nodded. "Yes, that's correct."

Lucia continued, "The spinning key also appeared when all the slime was on the lake. Coincidentally, or maybe not, the news said the city water pressure was reduced because of algae in the reserve water system. Mr. Tortosa, the richest man in town, was donating considerable money to help the city with the water problem. I remember his quote. He said, 'The aging water system will be a monster to repair, so I would like to help.' He referred to a monster."

"Like the slime-eating reptile and the tortoise that brought me to safety," breathed Anthony.

Kim responded in a commendatory voice, "That is a phenomenal insight! The spinning key also appeared at the end of the tug-of-war with Deep Dungeon. The boat crashed into the shore and threw a piece of shrapnel that tore a hole in Tug's flag, just like Anthony and Lucia's *Flying Hull Y'all* tore through the Finish Line banner at our Discovery Day boat race event."

"Oh, my," said Chelsea, "is the artificial intelligence system software in our glasses predicting the future? That's so unsettling! I need to ask my dad what in the world is going on."

"Whichever world it is," grumbled Dion.

That evening, Chelsea discussed all that had happened with her father. He frowned, remembering his previous suspicions about the capability of those glasses.

He looked noticeably upset. "This new information confirms it then. I will investigate this first thing tomorrow morning."

Looking at her father's troubled expression, she decided not to pursue it any further and headed off to her bedroom.

The following evening, after Chelsea's dad returned home from work, he had answers for his daughter.

The company he worked for was involved in several different artificial intelligence projects. Some of the development was quite advanced and as it turned out, the person who prepared the glasses for the gang gave them the wrong system software. Chelsea's dad learned it was software with security implications programmed to predict future events based on past knowledge and real-time inputs.

"The glasses that you and your friends have been given are driven by a powerful program capable of far-reaching imagination, innovation, and prediction," he said, as he sat down on the couch and provided more detail.

Chelsea replied, "Well, no wonder we've had such overwhelming experiences using them."

The next day, she told the gang what had happened. Everyone was relieved and a bit intimidated by the capability inside the artificial world of *The Lost View*.

Kim said, "We should agree to use these virtual reality glasses with extreme caution going forward."

Nate solemnly muttered, "The future is best left unknown."

Anthony had a little different perspective. He said, "The future remains unknown with or without the glasses. Even if we see the spinning key, we have no idea what it really means and if or how it will ever relate to our real lives. I think using the glasses has been an exciting experience that's taught us all something about the world around us and about ourselves."

"If we see the spinning key again when using the glasses, we should remember there may be an embedded message in that world that relates to something in our real lives," Lucia advised. "We have to be very careful and stop using the glasses if things get too weird."

Everyone agreed that was a good suggestion and decided to remain vigilant for the presence of the spinning key.

Kim was still considering a whopping virtual awards ceremony. She mentioned it to Lucia. "It would be quite entertaining for the seahorses and their jockeys to have such a celebration, even though none of us was declared the winner because of all the seahorse shenanigans. After all, in the virtual world, we can give away fantastic prizes for nothing. We never got the opportunity to celebrate the races as planned. I especially love parties."

Lucia thought for a minute, then replied, "That experience should be amusing."

So, they informed the rest of the gang and set a date for the following Wednesday for the gala affair.

Wednesday rolled around quickly. Everyone showed up at Kim's and put on their glasses.

Kim waved her hand before her glasses and said, "We're going to have an awards party for all who participated in the seahorse races."

Instantly, they could see Tug in the middle of Lake Moon Glow. He was all decorated for a celebration with streamers and signs congratulating the Aqua Jocks, as Anthony referred to them. All the seahorses were there, tied up to Tug. They were dressed for the occasion, and all seemed content. Poky was wearing a cowboy hat. Some of the others had colorful decorations on their Sandy's Saddles. Water Chestnut had the best tack, which included studded rhinestone reigns.

The sky was clear blue, and the sun reflected off small ripples in the lake. The trees along the shore bristled in the warm breeze blowing out of the west. It was indeed a fine day for an awards ceremony.

The gang could hear some strange noises that sounded something like jibber-jabber put to music.

"What could that be?" asked Kim.

Lucia responded, "You know, it looks like Ski Dattle is trying to sing."

"Oh my," said Chelsea. "I think he is trying to serenade Water Chestnut. He's looking straight at her."

"She seems to have no interest whatsoever," giggled Lucia.

"Well, so much for starting that special friendship," Dion chuckled. Then everyone laughed. "It appears that seahorse romance can be rather tenuous, just like humans," said Kim.

"Well, isn't that a relief? We're not the only ones," replied Lucia.

Kim had decided that all the jockeys and seahorses should get a prize of some sort, ranging from a large solid crystal bowl first-place trophy to season tickets to all the seahorse derby races in the future. Everyone was looking forward to finding out what they had won.

Suddenly, the sky turned gray as big dark clouds rolled across Moon Glow Lake.

Anthony commented, staring at the blackening heavens, "It almost looks like it's the middle of the night."

The wind picked up, lifting the congratulatory banners off Tug and cast them to the shoreline. Then the clouds opened, dumping torrential rains on the lake, drenching Tug and all the seahorses. Tug swayed from side to side as the wind tossed him about like a ball in a pinball machine trapped between two bumpers. Out of nowhere, the spinning key appeared in the lower right-hand field of view.

Chelsea said, "Look, everyone, there it is, the spinning key!"

This put the gang on edge.

"What's going on? This was no time for an awards ceremony, virtual or otherwise, especially with the spinning key in full view," said Kim, her brows furrowed.

As lightning struck down over Lake Moon Glow it lit up the sky so well the gang could see the squirrels on the far side of the lake scurrying to find cover. The following thunder seemed to shake the very ground everyone was standing on in Kim's basement. The entire experience was surreal.

Chelsea said in a fearful voice, "We need to suspend the ceremonies for the day right now and try again another time. Maybe."

Everyone quickly pulled off their glasses, returning to a safer reality among friends in the dark yet amiable basement.

Nate said, "I don't know what this terrible storm means, but I don't like it. The spinning key showed up just as the rain started. We all need to keep a lookout for bad weather."

"That's an understatement," commented Kim. "There is no telling what real-life events may have been signified this time by the spinning key. You saw how horrifying the clouds and rain were."

"I think we all need to relax," said Anthony. "I suggest we all go for ice cream and enjoy this warm sunny day in Sharefield Park."

"Now, there's a comforting idea!" Lucia said as she smiled in agreement.

Chatting among each other, the gang went off.

12

SCIENCE FAIR

The school's science fair was approaching, and everything else would take a backseat for the gang because they all wanted to participate. That very Wednesday afternoon after their intimidating virtual reality session, they sat eating their ice cream in Sharefield Park and started to discuss projects of interest.

"I like the idea of doing something with water conservation," Lucia said. "We have come to realize its importance in our everyday lives. I cannot imagine how serious things would become if we did not have access to all the water we need now and in the future."

Everyone agreed that that was the most relevant and provocative topic.

"I like the idea, but how are we going to construct a project around water ecology?" asked Nate.

Kim interjected, "We learned much about this life-sustaining resource on our Discovery Day, didn't we? That should give us a head start."

Chelsea commented, "Ms. Jenkins said that each project could not involve more than three students. That means that we will have to break up into two groups."

No one in the gang was enthusiastic about that idea, but with her take-charge attitude, Kim suggested, "Let's select the projects first and then decide who should be in which group."

"Okay," Dion said, "now we need some ideas."

Anthony replied, "This is not going to be easy. Maybe we can do something with seahorse nourishment in the ocean ecology."

"Very funny," said Chelsea. "We need something original and relevant to today's water supply and that of tomorrow."

"I have a thought," said Lucia. "During Discovery Day, we learned the difference between ice, drinkable water, and sea salt water. Maybe we can come up with a project related to the melting of glaciers."

Anthony responded, "That would be valuable, but setting up experiments around that topic would be difficult. We can't just head to the North Pole and set up camp. If we do something with ice melting, that would be rather mundane and not completely immersive, so to speak."

"Well then," said Kim, "maybe we can develop experiments related to saltwater, the heaviest of the three waters we learned about. It would be profound if we could magically transform saltwater into fresh drinking water."

"Actually, that is done every day. It is called desalination," Lucia explained. "I read that several Caribbean islands get all their freshwater by extracting salt from seawater. It is quite an operation."

"That project has the same problem as melting glaciers; we cannot exactly set up a desalination plant in Sharefield," said Dion. "Lake Moon Glow is already freshwater."

"This is true," said Nate, "but maybe we can do something on a very small scale. How is this desalination normally done anyway?"

Lucia seemed to know quite a lot about the topic and said, "There are a couple of methods. One is to chemically treat the water to cause the salt to be removed; the other method is called reverse osmosis. This method involves evaporating saltwater. The salt does not evaporate or turn to gas with the water. The evaporated water is captured and recondensed into liquid."

"This is why it rains," she continued. "Water that evaporates from lakes and oceans then forms clouds that cool in the higher altitudes and then rain down on us as freshwater.

The salt is not evaporated into the air with the water vapor in the first place, so it rains freshwater. Unfortunately, reverse osmosis is very energy intensive, meaning it takes a lot of energy to evaporate water. The sun offers incredible energy, but the method is not practical in many places. It is sometimes the best solution in areas near the sea where freshwater is not readily available."

Anthony was impressed. "That was a pretty darn good explanation, Lucia! I think that you are brilliant."

"Thank you," Lucia smiled. "It just happened to be something I learned about recently."

Kim asked, "How can we create something like this for a science project?"

Chelsea suggested, "We need a baby ocean to start with."

Dion said, "That might be something that we can come up with. We could get a small inflatable swimming pool and fill it with water, then add some salt."

Everyone said at once, "I like that idea."

Dion continued, "According to Lucia, once we have an ocean, we need a way to evaporate water, which will take a lot of energy."

"What do we have available to us that can give us a lot of energy?" asked Nate.

Anthony shook his head. "I have been sweating that question since Lucia told us just how much energy it would take."

Kim said, "Then perhaps you *have* come up with the answer. You said that you were sweating it. Sweat is our body's way of cooling off the sun's heat by evaporating water off our skin. According to Lucia, the sun has loads of energy, and it drives the formation of clouds and rain."

"Well then, maybe we can take advantage of the sun's energy to power evaporation in our baby ocean," Anthony interjected.

"That sounds very practical," said Dion. "Our teamwork is making this dream project come to life. The next step is figuring out how to collect the water vapor that evaporates off the surface of our salty swimming pool in the sun."

The Sharefield Gang did not have a good solution for that problem. They all agreed to think about it and then meet in the park again on Saturday to see if anyone came up with an idea.

That evening, Nate was thinking about the situation. He envisioned himself inside the problem as a tiny droplet of fresh water that had just emerged from the salty swimming pool, harnessed by the sun's energy. It seemed to him that there were a lot of ways to collect the evaporated water, but what would be the most practical among them?

He ended up really missing his friend Victor. He thought, *What would Victor suggest for a problem like this?* Victor was always organized and able to sort things out when there were a lot of possibilities. He had been staying in touch with his old friend, who had since moved to the west coast. He pulled out his phone, sent Victor a message about the gang's proposed science project, and asked him what he thought.

Victor got excited when he saw the text and immediately called Nate back. The two of them had a lot to talk about. Eventually, they got to the science project question of trapping the evaporated water from the swimming pool.

Victor said, "Coincidentally, there is a program to capture evaporated water from the sea off the coast close to where I live. It's a pilot program to determine if it would be efficient enough to be scaled up to provide freshwater for the coastal cities." He continued to elaborate, "You see, evaporated water is captured by enclosing large sea areas inside a huge transparent dome. The evaporated water condenses on the dome's walls and rolls down into a trough around its perimeter. The Romans used the same principle to recover evaporated water in their steam baths that were heated by hot rocks in ancient times." Nate said, "I find this all very interesting. Thank you, Victor, for the valuable insights. I will share all this information with the gang. Maybe we can come up with something similar," said Nate. Before they hung up, the two boys agreed to stay in touch regularly.

The following Saturday, the gang reunited in Sharefield Park as planned. Nate told everyone of the insightful conversation he had with Victor. "Victor said to say hello to everyone."

Dion replied, "We are all happy to hear he is doing well."

Nate said, "Yes, he is more than fine. He loves it out there on the coast. He told me that he visits the ocean all the time. He has made many new friends that hang out together on the beach."

Then Nate told the gang what Victor had shared about the saltwater desalination pilot project just off the coast.

"What a lucky coincidence," said Chelsea. "I wonder if we can build a dome over our salty swimming pool."

"Maybe we can cover our pool with clear plastic," Kim suggested.

Dion said, "The pool is a pretty good size; we will need some support structure to hold a flimsy plastic covering in the shape of a dome over the pool."

"How are we going to build that?" asked Anthony. "We can't just make it out of Tinkertoys."

Nate thought for a moment and then said, "Why not? We could connect them in a dome shape and glue them together with wood glue."

"That is an interesting thought," said Chelsea.

Then Lucia commented, "We could make a geodesic dome."

Anthony asked, "What in the world is a geodesic dome? It sounds like the name of a planet in a science fiction movie."

Lucia laughed. "Not at all. It is a way to connect supports in triangular shapes to make a very strong dome."

"Where do you get all of this useful information anyway?" Anthony wondered.

"I don't know," said Lucia. "I pick things up through what I read and experience. Then I try to remember them because I figure that some of it might be useful someday."

"That sounds like a very good strategy for solving problems," agreed Dion. "I try to do the same thing myself."

Nate said, "So if we make this wooden dome and cover it with plastic, it might be too heavy and sink to the bottom of the swimming pool. We need it on top so that we can collect the condensed water that rolls down the sides of the dome."

Dion thought for a moment. He randomly recalled the Majestic Mountain adventure from last summer. The Tree of Knowledge came to mind, and he thought of the image of a bicycle that was apparent in the wood grain of the trunk of that tree. *What an interesting coincidence that was*, he thought. Then, his mind drifted back to the problem of how to support a dome over the swimming pool of saltwater. Just like that, an idea popped into his head. "Maybe we can use a bicycle tire innertube filled with air around the dome to help it float," he suggested.

"That might be a possibility," said Kim. "How did you come up with that?"

"I don't really know," said Dion. "I happened to be thinking of last summer's adventures, and the idea just came to me."

Chelsea replied, "It might be a good idea, but a bicycle innertube will not be big enough to go around the swimming pool. The innertube needs to surround the entire outside of the dome to keep it balanced on top of the water. It would be hard to connect two of them and still have them hold air pressure."

Kim said, "We also need something to hold the condensed freshwater that rolls down around the inside perimeter of the dome and a way to remove it from the swimming pool so that we can measure it."

"The condensed water could roll down into a round trough at the base of the dome," said Anthony.

"Where do we get a round trough that is exactly the right size to fit around the inside of the dome?" asked Nate.

"That is a good question," said Anthony. "What else is there that floats that is sort of like a bicycle innertube that we can form around our dome?"

Kim replied, "A lifesaving flotation ring."

Lucia said, "That is a different idea, but it is also too small to fit around the swimming pool."

"I know," declared Dion. "What if we take a foam noodle, used for recreation and flotation in swimming pools, and wrap it around the outside of our dome? We can use two of them and attach them, end to end, using one of those exercise stretchy bands as a sleeve to wrap around the two pieces, joining them together."

"That is an ideal solution for outside the dome," said Kim. "We can cut them to the perfect length to match the circumference of our pool."

Then Lucia replied, "Some of those noodles have a hole through the center. We could cut one of that kind in half. The half-doughnut-shaped pieces can serve as our clean water collection troughs around the inside of the dome."

"Perfect!" said Anthony. "We can also cut those to the exact length and attach each section to the other to form a trough made out of foam on the inside of the dome."

Lucia added, "the tough needs to be sealed up watertight. Perhaps we can use some of the caulking left over from the names I wrote on our tie-dye tee shirts for the school play to seal the tub ends together."

"That makes sense," said Nate. "If the edges of the dome are set down inside the trough, the water will run off the plastic sheet covering our Tinkertoy frame directly into those half noodles."

Kim approved. "It looks like we have a complete workable design for a miniature desalination station!"

"Wait," cautioned Lucia. "We still need a way to get the water out of the trough inside the dome to measure it."

Chelsea said, "We could run a hose under the dome and into the trough."

"Yes, but we would have to pump the water out," Dion reasoned. "That would require a small pump and a battery to run it."

Nate was doubtful. This sounded like a whole new project.

Then Anthony chimed in, "We need two projects anyway. Maybe the pump and battery can be the second one."

Nate said, "That is not much of a project alone."

"Unless we make our battery that runs the pump from the extra salty water left in the swimming pool after we remove some freshwater from it," Anthony explained. "I saw a video online where a battery was made out of salt water."

"This sounds very interesting," cheered Chelsea. "Having a salt battery would make our system self-sustainable with no energy required except from the sun."

"I like that very much, too," said Kim. "It is a system of the future that does not require an external energy source to make freshwater."

"Okay, we can easily find a small aquarium pump to recover the fresh water. How do we make a salt battery to run it?" asked Dion.

"According to what I learned, we will need a few supplies like copper and zinc metal bars and some chemicals like hydrogen peroxide to add to the saltwater," said Anthony.

Kim said, "Now we can divide into two groups to work on these projects together."

Nate said, "I like to build models. The Tinkertoy dome is right up my alley." Dion said, "I would like to work with you on that."

Once she heard Dion, Kim responded immediately, saying, "The solar-powered desalination experiment also sounds like a good fit for me."

Anthony, Lucia, and Chelsea were all equally excited to build the apparatus for the salt-battery-powered pump that would remove the freshwater collected from around the swimming pool dome.

Dion remarked, "We are all committed to making these projects a huge success. We will experiment with and learn about water, the most valuable resource for all life on the planet. One that must be understood and managed into the future for the survival of all species on Earth."

"Well put!" exclaimed Lucia.

The following week at school, the Sharefield Gang approached Ms. Jenkins and told her about their joint science project ideas. Kim explained, "we will be working as two separate teams on projects that relate to each other."

Ms. Jenkins said, "I like the idea. You have my permission for the two groups to develop a water desalination system, provided each group collects their data and meets all the science fair requirements individually."

"We will do that," said Dion.

Everyone in the gang was thrilled to participate in these scientific studies. They were also looking forward to communicating with their old friend Victor, who was close to a real project that was a contributing inspiration for their own.

Nate said, "We all miss his friendship. Further, we all know that Victor will provide valuable insight into our projects' experimentation, data collection, and analysis methods."

13

BIRDS ON LAKE MOON GLOW

After working hard to figure out their science project, the gang wanted to take a break. They were curious to get back into the world of *The Lost View*, especially with the knowledge Chelsea had shared with them regarding their enhanced system's capabilities.

During their last session, they experienced a terrible storm on Lake Moon Glow while seeing the spinning key at the same time. This put the gang on edge again. It suggested the possibility of a natural disaster. Sharefield was not prone to excessive flooding in the past, but the spinning key must have meant something.

With this deeper understanding, the gang met once again in Kim's basement the following weekend to enter their world of *The Lost View*.

Chelsea said, "We have no idea what to expect."

As they slid the glasses over their eyes to enter their artificial world, Kim remarked, "More than ever before, we need to be aware of our surroundings in the virtual world and the associated potential consequences."

To their delight, the gang was looking out over a particularly sunny day on Lake Moon Glow. It helped them relax and made them feel warm inside.

"Things here are a bit more comforting after our last session," said Nate. "This is a welcoming break from the challenging school activities we have faced over the previous week." Then he noticed something in the shallow water on the far side of the lake. "I see something, but I cannot quiet make out what it is," he said. He waved his hand before his glasses and instructed them to zoom in on the unidentified object. The others followed his lead and did the same thing.

"What do you think we are looking at?" asked Kim.

"I'm not sure," said Nate, "but it looks like some sort of a giant bird."

Chelsea zoomed in closer and proclaimed, "It's a blue heron standing on one leg in the shallow water near the far edge of the lake."

"Yes, I see it now," said Lucia. "It has a huge neck and beak. It is dipping its head into the water, evidently trying to grab small fish for lunch."

Dion said, "It sure is a large bird. How does it manage to balance itself on only one leg?"

Anthony said, "It performs like it should be in the circus. Maybe we should call it the Magnificent Stupendous Amazing Exotic Dipping Blue Heron."

"How about we refer to it as Dip?" suggested Nate, rolling his eyes good-naturedly.

"That works for me," laughed Chelsea.

"If you insist," said Anthony. "He is Dippity Do Da to me."

Dip was having a delightful old-time feeding on small bluegills in the lake without a care. There was an abundance of them right where he was standing; he seemed to be gobbling them down one at a time as fast as he could swing such a large beak into the surface of the water.

Then, out of nowhere, there appeared something else flying around him.

Lucia said, "Look, I think it is a large insect."

She zoomed in on the flying object. It was moving so fast that she could not get a good look at it. Then suddenly, it stopped for a couple of seconds in midair, just in front of the threatening extended beak of the huge blue heron.

Lucia said, "I can hardly believe that it's hovering motionless, except for its wings, oscillating at a furious pace."

Lucia said, "Wait a minute, I can see that it has a green florescent neck reflecting the sunlight, a blueish head, and a long beak of its own. However, considerably smaller and dwarfed by that of the heron.

"It must be a hummingbird!" Kim exclaimed as she said it darted to the left and went out of sight.

"What a strange pairing, a hummingbird and a blue heron," noted Dion.

"Not exactly an even match," added Anthony.

As the gang watched, the hummingbird seemed to come and go in and out of view at an incredible speed.

Kim said, "Let's call it Buzz. It seems to be playfully buzzing that blue heron."

Once again, the hummingbird stopped just in front of Dip's beak. The two were beak to beak.

Dip was thinking that Buzz would make a fine dessert after an enjoyable lunch of the small bluegills plentiful in Lake Moon Glow.

Lucia said, "I don't believe the blue heron normally eats other birds, but it is certainly capable of catching and digesting them." Dip pulled its head back toward its body, forming an 'S' shape with its neck. Then it lunged toward Buzz like a coiled cobra snake striking its prey.

Blue herons are fast when feeding with their neck. Dip was exceptionally nimble. But just as Dip lunged toward Buzz with his long, sharp beak wide open, Buzz backed up almost at the speed of light and stopped again, still right in front of Dip as if to say, *I flap my wings at 50 times a second. I am the only bird on the planet that can fly backward—good luck trying to eat me!*

Then Buzz zoomed off again out of sight. The gang could see a large horned owl circling above from behind Dip. Few birds will attack the mighty blue heron because of its size, but a hungry, aggressive horned owl is the exception. Blue herons can see three times better than humans, but Dip did not notice the horned owl's stealthy attack from behind. Just before the strike, Buzz streaked across in front of the owl and distracted it just enough to abort its dive toward the blue hearing. As it turned upward, Dip got a good look at the potential adversary. Once Dip saw the horned owl, its advantage was lost. That owl quickly took off at its full speed of forty miles an hour in the opposite direction of the upset heron.

Buzz circled Dip slowly a couple of times as if to say, "I saved your life," as Dip slowly moved his head up and down in agreement. Then Buzz landed ever so briefly right on top of Dip's head. Everyone witnessed the newfound friendship between the two birds.

"Did you see that?" Chelsea exclaimed. "It was amazing!"

"Yes, I saw it. I am stunned," Lucia breathed.

"I noticed the spinning key was present in the lower right hand of our viewing area right when all of this was happening. What do you suppose that means?" said Dion.

"As we now know, that spinning key means some sort of prediction into the future," Dion advised. "We all need to be on the lookout for it, because this symbolism might manifest itself in our real lives."

Anthony smiled. "This is a strange one indeed. I guess sometimes we can all be a little flighty."

Kim added, "Let's just be careful and remain aware of what we just saw and how it might somehow come to fruition in our real world."

"Good advice, my kind friend," said Dion.

"This has been enough excitement for me for one day," said Chelsea. The gang agreed and ended their session in the world of *The Lost View.*

The following week, a nurse, who everyone referred to as Mr. Jay, came to the school. He gave a speech at the assembly on the value of working in the medical profession. He emphasized the satisfaction he and others like him received by comforting those in need. He asked the students to consider a career in the healthcare field so they, too, could experience some of the same rewards he spoke of. At the end of his presentation, he announced that anyone who would like to volunteer to visit the Sharefield Assisted Living Facility could go with him one day to meet some of the wonderful people there. He explained that many were elderly and needed medical and psychological care. He said interested students could engage with the staff and residents to experience caregiving firsthand.

His presentation touched Chelsea deeply. She lost her mother at an early age. Her dad has been very good to her. She knew how much he sacrificed on her behalf. Still, she missed not having a mother at home to talk with. She knew that her life was much different than that of her friends. She thought that visiting the assisted living facility might help her better understand what other people are going through and make her feel better about her situation. Chelsea, along with many of the other students, signed up to go with Mr. Jay.

As Chelsea boarded the school bus with the other students the morning of the field trip, she thought, *I am on a new adventure. There is no telling just where it will lead me.*

After a short ride across town, they were met at the door of the Sharefield Assisted Living Facility by a member of the staff. He filled the students in on the day's events. They were given a brief orientation and a tour of the facility. Afterward, each student was assigned a resident to spend some time with before returning to school in the afternoon. The students were asked to converse with their residents and learn all they could about their long life while sharing something about themselves simultaneously.

Chelsea was looking forward to this opportunity. She wanted to get the perspective of a senior who had lived a full life, perhaps to help her discover more about herself. After the tour, she was directed to room 217.

Chelsea was small for her age, the smallest of the gang, and not particularly strong. She was intimidated when she entered the room to find a very husky six-foot-seven-inch elderly gentleman sitting in the chair directly before her. He invited her in to sit in the seat facing him. As she did so, she felt self-conscious. Her chair and his were very close together. The man introduced himself in a deep, hollow voice. "Hello, my name is Fred Thornton."

Chelsea replied, "Hi, I am Chelsea."

Fred said, "I heard someone was going to visit me today. I don't get a lot of visitors."

Chelsea said in a low voice, "I see."

Then Fred raised his voice. "You have to speak up, young lady. I don't hear as well as I used to."

Chelsea was a bit taken aback, but she was on a mission to learn about this man and had been told that communication could be difficult with some of the residents who may be struggling in one way or another.

So, she pressed on in a louder voice. "How long have you lived here, Mr. Thornton?"

"About two years," said Fred. "And please, call me by my first name."

"All right," said Chelsea. "It is nice to meet you, Fred."

As the conversation continued, Chelsea found out that Fred's wife had died about five years ago and that their two grown children and four grandchildren had moved out of state. He saw them only a couple of times a year.

Chelsea said, "It's a shame that you do not get to see your family very often."

Fred nodded. "I get very few visitors. You are the first in several months."

Chelsea could hardly imagine not having visitors regularly. She may not have her mother to talk with, but she was afforded special time with her dad every day, not to mention her bonding friendship with the Sharefield Gang.

"How do you spend your time?" asked Chelsea.

"I like to watch sports on TV, especially football," Fred answered.

"I like sports, too. I plan to play on the girls' softball team during the summer. I don't really know a lot about football, though."

"Football is a tough sport. I should know. Do you see this ring?" Fred held up his hand to show a huge gold ring filled with diamonds on the third finger of his right hand.

"Yes, I noticed it as soon as I walked in. It's gorgeous."

"It is a Super Bowl ring. We were world champions that year. I played defensive tackle. We won that game on defense. Our front line would not let anyone through. You can't win a game if forced to pass every play."

"Wow!" beamed Chelsea. "What an accomplishment."

"Well, everything in life comes at a price, young lady. These days, I have my memories but not much more. Some days are very long, and I don't always feel well."

Chelsea could see the sadness in his large, dark eyes and asked, "Do you think I could come to visit you again sometime?"

"I would like that," nodded Fred, gravely.

It was about time for Chelsea to meet up with her classmates and return to school on the bus. She said goodbye to Fred and promised to visit him again soon.

Returning to school, she thought about what her visit meant to Fred. She remembered the blue heron and hummingbird she and the gang encountered in their last session of *The Lost*

View. Now she knew why the spinning key was present in that scene. The symbolism of the sequence of events from their previous virtual reality session played out in real life with her and Fred. She realized that just small acts of kindness can make a huge difference in the lives of others.

She promised herself that she would make time to go back and see Fred. *Perhaps others in the gang will join me occasionally,* she thought. *After all, it is not every day that you get to meet a professional football player, especially one with a Super Bowl ring!*

Later that afternoon, Chelsea told the Sharefield Gang about her day and her exchanges with Fred. Everyone was touched. The entire gang decided to join Chelsea on her next visit to see Fred the following weekend. During that visit they all shared stories ranging from sports to the future of artificial intelligence.

There was an emotional moment when Fred was talking about his Super Bowl victory, when he said, "It means a lot to me just to be able to talk about my past with others. In some ways, Chelsea and the rest of your friends are a lifesaver to me." The friends were touched by his comments.

Over the next few weeks, the gang regularly visited Fred. His health was gradually deteriorating. He was starting to forget simple things. As time went on, the gang noticed he was becoming more forgetful. However, he always looked forward to visits from the gang. They always cheered him up. One staff member told Chelsea that Fred's condition consistently showed improvement the day after their visit.

He told her, "There is much more to one's overall health than physical aspects. One's emotional frame of mind contributes significantly to one's overall health."

Chelsea replied, "I always feel a lot better myself after visiting with Fred. I am worried about him. Is there anything more we can do for him?" she asked. "There isn't much any of us can do. It is a part of the natural aging process. I realize that this is something that you are not accustomed to thinking about as a strong young adult."

One day in late spring, the gang arrived for a surprise visit at the assisted living facility. Walking down the hall approaching Fred's room, they sensed something was wrong.

Chelsea said, "Look, Fred's door is closed. It is always left open. What is going on?"

As they came to the door, Dion knocked on it. His knuckles against the hollow core door echoed down the hallway. There was no answer.

Kim said, "Try to turn the knob or push it, maybe?"

Dion tried to turn the doorknob, but the door was locked. Chelsea looked at it blankly.

Coming down the hall toward them was the head nurse at the facility. They had come to know her as Nurse Donna over the past few months. She stopped and spoke. "I have some sad news for you." The gang all knew what she was going to say. "Fred passed away of natural causes during the night. I am sorry. He gave us all such joy. We will miss him."

"This is a hard thing to swallow," said Chelsea.

"Think of what he shared with you as a gift. You meant a lot to him and helped him more than you know. One of the caregivers said she found a note inside his nightstand. He wrote it a couple of weeks ago."

Nurse Donna handed the note to Chelsea. The note from Fred was addressed to the Sharefield Gang. Chelsea's hands were shaking as she opened the folded looseleaf paper and read it out loud. Her voice cracked as the words struggled out of her mouth.

Thanks to the Sharefield Gang for showing me such profound and genuine kindness. Such is a gift valued more than any other. Please allow me to return the favor with a little advice. Use your talents to create a better world.

It was signed simply with the name, your friend, Fred. Chelsea read the note aloud a second time with more composure. She ended it by saying, "Fred will surely be missed, but we are fortunate to have enjoyed his companionship. He gave more to us than he probably realized. He taught me not to judge too quickly and to live in the present moment."

Kim said, "I learned something about humility. Fred was a renowned football superstar yet was so personable and genuine with us."

Lucia added, "We all learned the value of our close relationships. Our gang shares that closeness."

Everyone agreed.

As Chelsea held the note, Kim said, "Look, on the back of the note, Fred has drawn an image of a key."

Chelsea turned the note over and saw the drawing. "It is similar to, but different than, the key that we see in our world of *The Lost View*. How could Fred have known what that key even looked like?"

Dion replied, "Well, Chelsea, you may not know the whole story of that key. I had a similar key that was a big part of our lives last year before you moved to Sharefield. That is a story to be told another day. I showed my key to Fred one day during a visit I had with him by myself."

"Fred was very impressed with the key and held it in his large hands for most of our visit. Before giving it back to me, he said he wanted to remember it. His ability to recall things at that time was deteriorating every week. Perhaps he made this drawing so that he could let us know that he remembered the key. I had told him just how much it had influenced our lives and that he was profoundly influencing all of us as well."

Chelsea replied, "Really, maybe he was trying to tell us that he has some relationship to the key?"

"I guess anything is possible," said Nate.

"We may never know for sure," said Kim.

Fred's celebration of life was a very private affair attended only by his immediate family. The gang each paid their respects in their own way and remembered their short time with him.

14

THE SCIENCE EXPERIMENTS

In between school, homework, and visits with Fred, the gang was just getting started on their science projects.

Their lives were busy, and they had no time to waste. They knew that the science projects would be quite consuming. The gang really wanted to excel at them.

They first had to collect all the materials for the experiments, so they got together in Sharefield Park one Saturday to make a list of things they would need to build their models. It was a rather odd list of varied materials, from Tinkertoys to foam water floats, an aquarium pump, copper, zinc bars, etc.

Dion told the group, "Making a list will keep us organized so that we don't forget anything as we gather parts together. We will have everything on hand when we begin construction of our models. I learned this from Victor."

Everyone knew Victor loved making lists and being organized.

Soon after finishing it, Nate contacted their old friend Victor again to see if he had anything to add to the list. Victor always said that having a list helped him move things forward. As it turned out, after Nate mentioned the project to Victor a few weeks back, he made arrangements to tour the real pilot desalination project just off the coast near his family's home. Victor said that the tour was fascinating. He and other students were given a full rundown of the operation. Victor told Nate that it was state-of-the-art technology. He offered to email the gang some photos he had taken during his tour.

Nate said, "That would be fantastic. The pictures and your descriptions will help us understand the operation."

Nate was jubilant to have Victor's input and knew that the rest of the Sharefield Gang felt the same way. He asked Victor to be an unofficial advisor to their science projects. The knowledge he gained during his recent experience at the desalination pilot plant inspired all.

Victor was more than happy for the opportunity to get involved with his old friends. Nate explained the design they had devised to use solar energy to desalinate water and how they would use some of the resulting saltwater to make a battery that would run a pump to remove the distilled water from the collection trough. Victor was quite impressed and said that, in principle, it should work the same way as the pilot system he had recently had the opportunity to visit.

Nate asked Victor if there was anything that might be missing or was incorrect in their thinking.

"What if it rains during your experiment?" Victor asked. "Won't the rainwater dilute the exposed water in your swimming pool outside the dome and throw off your results?"

Nate said, "You are absolutely correct. I knew that you could help us."

After Nate told the rest of the gang about Victor's concern, they decided to cover the perimeter of the pool area, outside of the dome, with additional plastic to prevent rainwater from getting into the pool. At the same time, Lucia suggested, "Maybe we should put some weight around the dome so that it does not blow off if the wind picks up."

"That is thinking ahead," said Nate. They found some wood planks that they could lay over the gap between the edge of the inflated swimming pool and the foam ring around the dome.

The gang had collected everything they needed to build their science project models and begin their experiments. They got together each night after school that week to work on the models. Making a geodesic dome out of Tinkertoys was the hardest part. They needed a form over which to construct the dome to be the correct round shape. Kim's mother had a large exercise ball that she let them use. They over-inflated it to be large enough to serve as a form for their dome. Chelsea, Dion, and Nate glued the Tinkertoys to make the dome over the ball. Dion removed the ball once the glue was dry and covered the stiff dome structure with clear plastic. By the end of the week, they had completed the model of their desalination experiment.

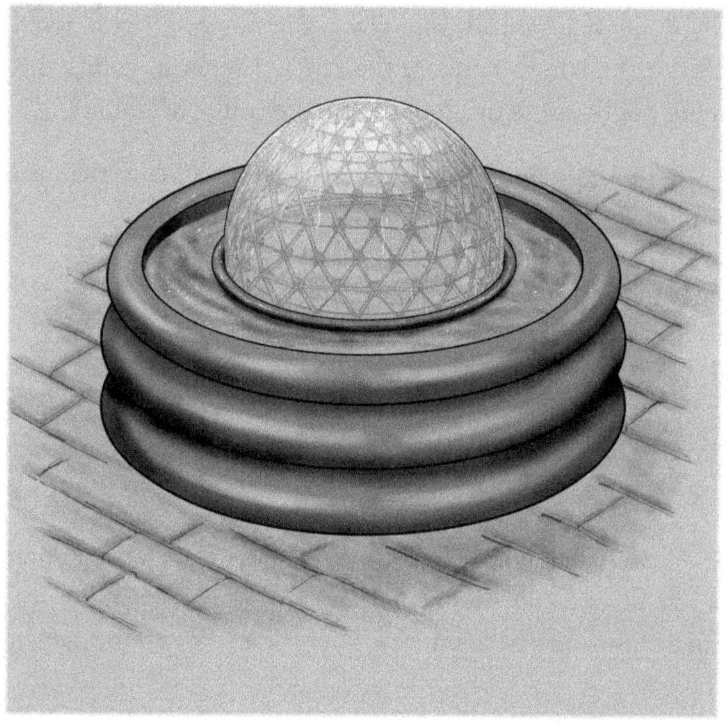

Anthony, Lucia, and Chelsea found a large bucket and attached the zinc and copper electrodes to each side with binder clips used to hold thick stacks of paper. As a pretest, they filled their bucket with salt water and stirred in hydrogen peroxide. They were able to run the aquarium pump and move freshwater through a tube from one glass to another.

The models were all complete. Before they could begin their experiment, they needed to determine how they would collect data most accurately to make the results they obtained meaningful.

After some discussion, the gang set up the test at Chelsea's house.

She commented, "Let's put the swimming pool on the sunny patio to the side of the house so it will not kill the grass. The patio faces south. That will offer the best exposure to the sun over the entire day."

"Good idea," said Nate. Kim suggested, "How about we run the test for two weeks?" Everyone felt that was about the right amount of time.

Thinking aloud, Lucia said, "So we add a measured amount of salt to the pool water before the test then check it daily. We should record the average daytime temperature because that will influence the amount of evaporation. Then, in the evenings, the condensed water is pumped off using the battery from a bucket of saltwater collected and measured from the pool the previous day."

"Yes, that all makes sense," said Anthony. "The amount of condensed water collected each day should be weighed. We can determine the salt content of the water used to run the pump by timing how long the salt battery will run."

"How do we do that after we have pumped all the freshwater out of the trough for the day?" asked Chelsea. "I guess that after we pump all the condensed water out, we can time pumping extra clean water from one bucket to another until the pump stops. This way, we, on the battery team, can fully account for the time the pump ran each day from the salt water taken out of the pool the day before."

After the gang worked out all these procedures Kim commented, "Wow, this is all rather complicated. Together we figured out a proper way to collect the data."

Lucia agreed and suggested, "Why don't we meet at Chelsea's house at the same time each evening to record the data?"

Chelsea said, "That would be fantastic. We can all work together as two teams on our experiments."

Dion told Kim and Nate, "I will be the note-keeper for our group since we will have to document and graph the results after we finish the experiment."

"Dion, you will be providing a tremendous service for all of us if you can do that," Kim acknowledged.

"I will do the same for our group," offered Lucia.

Chelsea and Anthony were both grateful.

As Anthony remarked, "Lucia, you are so nice and smart too."

Lucia did not know what to say but smiled in approval.

Everyone met at Chelsea's house on the first evening of the experiment. It was a bright, sunny day with little cloud cover. The gang could see the water collected in the channel around the inside of the dome.

"This is exciting," said Nate.

After getting the day's average temperature for Sharefield from a weather app on their phones, Chelsea and Lucia got the bucket of salt solution they set aside yesterday when they initially filled the pool with saltwater.

After connecting everything up Chelsea turned on the switch. The pump began to run as fresh water from the circular trough traveled through a tube out of the dome and into a container so that it could be weighed. After all the water was out of the trough, according to procedures, the team continued to let the pump run. They pumped extra clean water from another bucket powered by the saltwater battery until it stopped running.

Dion recorded the weight of the freshwater removed from the dome while Lucia wrote down the time the pump ran from power supplied by the saltwater battery.

Each day, they repeated this process. By the fourth day they were starting to realize a trend.

Lucia said, "The water in the swimming pool must be getting saltier as the freshwater is being removed because our saltwater battery is running the pump longer each day from the pool water removed the day before."

Together, Dion and Lucia kept very good notes of every part of the experiment.

By the start of the second week, it had only rained one day. Victor's suggestion to cover the exposed area of the pool outside of the dome proved to be very useful. Although they got no freshwater that day because there was no sunshine, they avoided diluting their salt pool with additional fresh rainwater.

Everyone had just arrived at Chelsea's house on the twelfth day to take their experiment readings. By this time, the procedures were all becoming quite routine. Just before they were to go out to the patio, the gang heard a loud squill followed by sharp, repetitive barking.

"That is Grand Paw!" said Chelsea.

He was barking like there was something wrong with him. The gang ran out to see just what was going on. There he was, sitting next to the bucket of salt water drawn from the pool the day before. It was the water for the battery to run the pump that evening.

"Oh," said Chelsea, "Grand Paw must have tried to drink our saltwater and got a mouth full of that salty stuff."

Chelsea moved to comfort her dog, and just as she did, his huge paw swung across the bucket and knocked it over.

"Oh no!" cried Anthony. "That is our experimental water bucket. Now, what are we going to do?"

Dion said, "You know, the amount of freshwater we have been recovering from the pool has decreased each day as the water gets saltier. We only have two days to go. I vote that we end our experiment today and take a final reading of the remaining water in the pool."

Kim agreed. "You have a good point. The decision to run the experiment for exactly two weeks was arbitrary. A dozen days is just as good. Sometimes, you must adjust your plans based on unexpected circumstances."

Chelsea replied, "I am just glad that Grand Paw did not knock over the bucket of water on one of the first days of the experiment."

Nate said, "We will take the good luck."

Over the following days, the gang met in Kim's basement to draw conclusions from their experiments and prepare for their oral presentation. They enjoyed sharing the information with Victor, who always had something to add based on his trip to a real desalination plant. After the display boards were together with graphs and charts, the gang practiced giving their oral presentation. Each of them had a section to present. They worked at it until everyone felt comfortable with their part. The presentations were well polished by this point.

"This is just like our theater performance," remarked Chelsea.

"Only this time we will be questioned by the judges," said Lucia.

Then I will give you a trial run," said Anthony. "This ought to be good," replied Lucia.

Anthony asked, "Why is salt white?"

Lucia protested, "The judges will not ask me that."

"I want to know," persisted Anthony.

Lucia said, "I think that it is because visible light does not have enough energy to pass through it, so it bounces off."

"Oh, like my head," said Anthony.

"I might agree that nothing will pass through your head sometimes, but you have a soft heart."

Finally, the big day for the presentations had arrived. The science fair was held on a Saturday afternoon at Central High School.

The two teams of the Sharefield Gang set up their displays next to each other. Everyone was well-rehearsed and ready to present their part.

A couple of students who were showing a chemical reaction displayed the science fair entry next to the desalination experiment. They used a heater to enhance the reaction and make it happen quicker for the judges.

The hot air from the heater was blowing directly on Kim, Dion, and Nate as they reported their results to the judges.

Kim said, "That heat blowing on me while I spoke was terribly distracting. I did my best to concentrate but left out a few things and stumbled over one of the judge's questions. I hope that it does not influence our score."

"Don't worry about it, Kim," said Dion. We did the best we could under the circumstances. I made a mistake as well. His words comforted her.

"Sometimes we just must accept things out of our control." Nate replied, "One thing is for certain: the judges could not have missed that we put much thought and effort into this project. All of that must count for something of value."

The gang was proud of all their work and felt they covered all aspects of their project well. They excelled at everything from the design of their model, its construction, the data collection, and the analysis of the results. None of the judges even asked them why the experiment was only run for twelve days. After all, the water in the pool had gotten so salty it was a natural stopping point for the experiment anyway.

Anthony, Chelsea, and Lucia also impressed the judges with their thorough analysis of the salt-powered battery.

The chemistry experiment beside them was next to be evaluated. The students had cranked the temperature of the heater up too high. It pointed at the desalination experiment table and blew its display board over. The students with the chemistry project saw what was happening and angled the heater up toward the ceiling to avoid directing the hot air over the gang's display. Suddenly, water started raining down on Kim, Dion, and Nate's desalination display. It was pouring rain and soaking everything! That heater from the display next to theirs had activated the sprinkler in the ceiling, causing it to rain on the gang as they stood in front of their soaked display table.

Everyone laughed. They had already given their presentation, and the water was a fitting end to their project. Chelsea remarked that she remembered the ferocious rain during the world of *The Lost View* session when they were supposed to give out the rewards for the seahorse race.

"The spinning key was present when it rained on our virtual world that day," she reminded her friends. "Now it is raining here as we are about to be judged for our science projects."

Yes," said Dion. "Another virtual event is coming true."

Unlike the virtual rainstorm that ruined their award ceremony, both teams in the Sharefield Gang were presented with the highest honor ribbons for their work on their desalination station and saltwater-powered clean water recovery system, despite the distractions. They were elated. It reinforced in them the power of teamwork to accomplish incredible things.

As soon as they left the school with their ribbons, they contacted Victor to share the news. He commended them on their success.

Nate said, "You are a part of our success. We all thank you for your valuable insights." Victor replied, "I am grateful you have given me the chance to interact with my friends, the Sharefield Gang. It was just like the good old days."

15

RETURN TO VIRTUAL REALITY

The Sharefield Gang decided to have one last session in their world of *The Lost View* to help them complete their review of the glasses and the artificial intelligence that fabricated and perpetuated their virtual world. The friends met in Sharefield Park on Saturday morning to discuss their final encounter with the glasses before returning them to Chelsea's dad.

They wanted to make sure they were prepared for whatever might happen. They knew that the spinning key in the lower right corner of their view would mean that the intelligence in the system was giving them obscure predictions of the future. Because they knew this, they were apprehensive even to attempt to use the glasses again. Yet, they felt that there was something left unfinished in the world of *The Lost View.*

They wanted to bring closure to the experience that had shaped so much of their tenth-grade year and changed the way that each one of them saw the world around them. So, they discussed the upcoming adventure under their favorite big oak tree in the park.

Chelsea started the conversation by reminding everyone that their world of *The Lost View* was not real. "Even though the artificial intelligence algorithm has been able to pull together enough information from all the data that it has been given to predict fragments of what might happen in our future, it is not real. It is still just a machine that recognizes patterns from the vast amount of data it has received and then uses those patterns by assuming that they will be closely replicated in one form or another."

"That may all be true," Dion noted, "but the circumstances were so vivid as we interacted in real-time with our world of *The Lost View.* It has done remarkably well, revealing situations that have become relevant to our future. Although not precisely correct in all instances, it has been close enough to be impactful. For example, the system may have saved my life from that speeding car. I delayed crossing the street because I saw that monarch butterfly on the cosmetic truck down the street from the crosswalk."

Anthony said, "I wonder where all of this artificial intelligence will go in the future."

"I don't know," said Lucia, "but it cannot think like each of us as individuals."

"Why not?" asked Nate. "It seems pretty smart."

"We are who we are because of everything we have experienced through our five senses," explained Lucia. "That, combined with our genetic makeup, pushes us to be prone to be one way or another. And, as we have learned, we continue to grow with each input we receive from our senses. These inputs allow us to think, and act based on logic and intuition. All these factors together make each of us unique."

Kim agreed. "I guess that is true. A machine that digests tons of information beyond what we can know or remember has some unique advantages over us in solving certain problems, but it has not experienced a lifetime of emotions, along with taste, touch, smell, hearing, and, of course, seeing. It will not have the same internal data that each of us uniquely has, combined with our physical makeup, that collectively makes us uniquely who we are. You can tell a machine what pain and joy are, but it is not the same as feeling them. Our reactions to such emotions may not always be the same as a machine's data-based response."

"Yes, but there must be a lot of value in knowing so much about so much and being able to find patterns in all of that information when posed with a question," added Nate.

"That is for sure," said Chelsea. "My dad has told me of many beneficial things artificial intelligence is just beginning to do. In the future, it will offer a tremendous service to humankind. Artificial intelligence is not something to fear.

Throughout history, new technologies have been feared simply because they are new. In general, we humans do not always like change." Anthony said, "I read where there was a good market for fake horse heads that fit on the front of the first automobiles because people had a hard time accepting that dramatic change in transportation. It scared them. The horse head made the car less threatening."

"Similarly, artificial intelligence is scary because we do not yet know its limitations. In time, we will further appreciate its value to us," said Lucia." It has shown us that it is very good at assimilation. A large part of creativity is assimilation, but not all. The decision to rank what is relevant is a human endeavor particular to the creator. Artificial intelligence cannot perform this task specifically like each of us as individual creators would."

Kim replied, "So, the art of the future will take for granted an almost infinite knowledge base from which to draw insight and will concentrate on the relevance of choices specific to the creator."

"I agree with that," said Dion. "Sometimes these human choices will be emotionally based, and at other times they may be more strategic as determined by circumstances, but they will not be random. They will be more than a best guess based on the past. They will be the ones most relevant to the author's work, whatever that might be."

Now that the gang had discussed the relevance and limitations of artificial intelligence, they felt ready to enter the world of *The Lost View* one last time. They met in Kim's basement on Tuesday after dinner for the experience.

As they put on their glasses, they were all quite confused. They found themselves in the Caribbean on an island beach.

"How did we end up here?" asked Dion. "I expected to see Lake Moon Glow, Tug, and our seahorses. We did not scan anything like this into the system. This is very puzzling."

There were surfboards for everyone, so the gang decided to try them. The water was a beautiful emerald green, and the waves curled onto the shore, offering the perfect conditions for surfing.

"Look," Chelsea observed, "the key is in the right-hand corner."

Everyone saw it, but it was different this time. It was positioned in the astrolabe as it was when Chelsea noted it in the video of this year's school play, *The Caribbean Adventure*. As Chelsea had witnessed, the arrow was spinning about its axis very fast. The key details were not clear enough to be made out by anyone at this considerable rotational speed.

No one really knew what to make of it. Was artificial intelligence possibly creating a new virtual reality related to the specific events of this year's school play?

As the gang entered directly into the world of *The Lost View* and grabbed their surfboards, they looked at each other and realized they all looked at least five years older.

"Could it be that the artificial intelligence is telling us that we will all be enjoying this for real someday?" asked Lucia.

"That would be so cool!" said Anthony.

Kim agreed. "Yes, I would like that very much as well."

"Kim and I would have a good time together surfing on this island paradise," said Dion.

Just then, someone came running out of the bathhouse toward the gang as they picked up their surfboards and started getting ready to enter the water. As this person approached, his stride looked strangely familiar. The closer he got, the more the gang felt a connection. Yet, it was not someone they had scanned into their system when building the visual database for the world of *The Lost View*.

Then he yelled, "Hello, everyone!"

That voice was unmistakable. It was Victor. As he approached, everyone could see that it was indeed him, just a few years older like the rest of them.

"This is so cool!" said Kim. "Victor, seeing you again in our artificial world is wonderful."

Everyone agreed and shared a hug with Victor, who was grinning from ear to ear.

He said, "I am so happy to see you all here!"

The seven friends started toward the water to enjoy the surf and get in a little practice. After they got a feel for the waves and the sport of surfing, everyone could stand on their board and ride toward the shore. It was such a thrill!

As lunchtime approached in their virtual world, they decided to go up to the boardwalk in front of the beach and see if they could find someplace to enjoy lunch together. They saw a table set up in the sand as they entered the beach after one last fantastic ride. On it was the crystal trophy intended for the seahorse race winner from several sessions ago. They were all surprised to see it. Nate explained to Victor what the trophy was for, all that had happened on Lake Moon Glow that led up to the final seahorse race, and the decision not to award the trophy to anyone.

"Maybe we are supposed to have a surfing competition and award the beautiful crystal trophy for this event," suggested Kim.

"That makes perfect sense," said Chelsea. "It sounds like the ideal way to celebrate this day together and bring closure to our previous escapades."

Nate said, "Most definitely, but first, let's see if any place serves food along the boardwalk. Then we can return to the beach and determine which of us is the top surfer."

They were not sure that there would be other people around, given that, until now, the artificial intelligence system was incapable of creating interactive human figures completely on its own. The gang reasoned that since Victor was in their thoughts and words regularly while they were in the world of *The Lost View*, where they would reference him often, the system was able to pick up enough information on him and bring him into their world in some form or another for this reunion. However, creating other individuals completely from scratch, out of nowhere, was a different story altogether.

As the gang walked up the beach, they did indeed see a thriving commercial area. There was a tee-shirt shop, a surf-board shop, and a diner just half a block away.

"This is strange," said Dion.

Nate replied, "I wonder who, if anyone, is tending to these places."

"There is only one way to find out," said Lucia.

She turned off the boardwalk and headed directly into a jewelry store.

"That was brave," noted Anthony. "Come on, let's follow her."

So, everyone headed through the door with her. Behind the counter, there was indeed a person waiting to greet them.

"Hello," said Lucia.

The lady opened her arms over the display case and greeted everyone, saying, "Hello, how can I help you?"

The gang was shocked. They had convinced themselves that this was probably not even possible. Kim was skeptical. To her, the voice of the store assistant sounded somewhat mechanical. Then she realized that the associate was wearing dark glasses. It was not exactly like the special ones she was wearing in real life, but they were still glasses. Glasses that could perhaps be displaying an artificial world for her.

Kim whispered to Dion, "Do you think she is real?"

"What do you mean?" asked Dion.

Kim replied, "Well, she is wearing glasses."

Dion shrugged, so Kim continued, "Maybe she is an artificial person in our world of *The Lost View,* living in her own artificial world."

"You mean like a robot?" asked Dion.

"Well, yes, sort of, I guess. A futuristic robot," Kim explained. Then she thanked the lady behind the counter as she and Dion hastily grabbed the arms of their friends and rushed them out of the jewelry store back onto the boardwalk as fast as they could.

There, Kim explained her theory to the others. "Maybe the people here are robots of the future living inside of their own virtual world. They all live and work from the same database, but it is not as extensive as ours. It is limited to their assigned operation of various tasks."

Just then, a man figure walked down the street, wearing dark glasses like the lady in the jewelry store.

"See?" said Kim. "He is wearing the same glasses. We know from Chelsea and her dad's explanation that artificial intelligence uses massive amounts of data to make correlations and then extrapolate them to create new similar situations. What if the people here in our future world of *The Lost View*

were created from the massive data and correlations collected on how humans act and work? Maybe they are inside their own world, functioning from limited, although quite massive, data. Perhaps they interact with each other in their own virtual world."

"But why?" asked Anthony. "Who started this side culture of robotic humans in the first place?"

"Maybe humans did," suggested Lucia.

Chelsea said, "My dad always speaks of the value of robots of the future that will serve us. Maybe this is how they have evolved, so to speak, if I can use that term."

"So let me get this straight," said Nate. "The humans we see are not real. They are robots living in an artificial world driven by a huge database that we humans created for our benefit so that they can serve us. Right now, we are in our artificial world of *The Lost View*, observing this robot culture at some time in the future."

"That sounds about right," said Dion. "As bizarre as it may be to us at this time."

Just ahead was a hamburger restaurant. Anthony suggested, "Let's see if a robot inside can make us a burger."

Sure enough, as they walked into the establishment, two human-looking robots stood facing them, both wearing the same glasses. The gang each ordered customized burgers with fries. Several other very efficient human-looking robot cooks working and singing in the kitchen prepared them in no time.

Victor commented as they ate their delicious lunch, "This is simply amazing. It is wonderful to be here with you guys."

The gang was all feeling his presence. It was almost too real to be artificially induced. Nate was so overwhelmed by the experience that he had to slip off his glasses for a few seconds to confirm he was still in Kim's basement and Victor was not there.

After lunch, the gang returned to the beach for the surfing competition. Everyone was looking forward to it. During lunch, they decided that each surfer would be given three attempts to ride a wave. They could all use the same wave if they wished. After the competition, the surfer with the longest combined time on their board would be awarded the beautiful crystal trophy sitting on the table in the sand.

16

SURFING COMPETITION

As the seven of them grabbed their boards and ran through the sandy beach into the crisp blueish-green ocean, they were energized with excitement and anticipation of victory. The gang paddled out together to catch their first wave. Dion and Nate grabbed a vicious one coming right at them. They both were able to get up onto their boards. Nate rode that raging wave farther into shore than Dion, temporarily putting him first, but not for long. The girls and Anthony and Victor picked up a near-perfect monster wave at just the right instant. It was a good ride for all of them, moving Chelsea into first place. As the afternoon wore on, everyone in the gang moved onto shore, riding various waves, then back out again. The surfing conditions were ideal. It wasn't easy to keep track of who was where.

Later, the gang was all out in the water together nearing the end of the afternoon, waiting for that one special killer wave. The one that only comes by when you least expect it. There it was, coming toward them. Just then, Dion spotted something strange and most unexpected. He pointed and said, "Who is that already up on his board riding the wave doing tricks like a gymnast on the parallel bars? Nate replied, "We have not seen him out here today. This guy is in a class of his own. But just who is he?" After he flew past them, they lost sight of the trick surfer.

Anthony asked, "Was that some kind of artificial robot expert surf bum?"

After the gang finished their last wave of the day, they discussed their cumulative time on the board as they walked toward the table with the trophy.

Standing beside the table was that other surfer they saw in the water who had outclassed every one of them. Sure enough, he was wearing glasses, but they differed from the other robots they had seen on the boardwalk. These glasses looked more like regular sunglasses.

He was a strong, well-built man who looked rather intimidating. As they approached him, he said nothing but appeared to be eyeing the beautiful crystal trophy on the table. The Sharefield Gang was having trouble figuring out who had won the competition, but they all realized that this guy, whoever he was, was a far better surfer than any of them.

Before reaching the table, they decided that the trophy should belong to the mystery surfer. He had earned it.

Kim said to Dion, "We all agree, you tell him that the trophy is his." Just before they reached the table, they saw the key spinning in the astrolabe in the lower right-hand corner of their field of view again. Like before, the key resembled a spinning top, making it difficult to discern its features.

As they reached the table, Dion wasted no time picking up the trophy and presenting it to the stranger, saying, "This is for you. You are the best!"

The mysterious surfer smiled and took hold of the trophy with one hand, then dropped his glasses with the other.

Very strange, Lucia thought. *He looks like a regular person.* Without saying anything, he reached out and shook Dion's hand. He had very large hands, indeed. Dion felt his knuckles scrunch together by the strength of his grip.

Then he just walked off toward the edge of the beach where a motorcycle was parked. He pulled a set of keys out of his pocket. Before he started the bike, he raised his hand and waved goodbye to the gang. His keys were in his hand. Everyone could see that there was an extra key on his key ring. It looked like the key found on stage from last year's play. The same key that fit into the astrolabe in this year's theater production. The same key that kept appearing in the world of *The Lost View*. Yet, it was different. It had the same shape but a different design on its face. No one knew what this could mean. Then the stranger lowered his hand, stuck the bike key into his cycle, twisted it, kicked it into gear, and quickly drove out of sight.

"That was weird," said Anthony.

Chelsea shivered. "That was more than weird. That was *scary* weird. He reminded me so much of Fred."

Lucia gasped, "When he shook Dion's hand, I saw the Super Bowl ring. He was wearing it."

"Who is Fred?" asked Victor.

Chelsea explained that Fred was an elderly man who had lived at the Sharefield Assisted Living Facility and had been their friend. "But how did he end up in our world of *The Lost View?*" she asked.

Victor replied, "Well, I showed up here through your multiple references to me. Did you ever speak of or interact with Fred in your virtual world?"

"I am certain that we spoke of him on more than one occasion," said Kim.

"Well, maybe, just maybe, that was his grandson, coming into our world of *The Lost View*," Lucia suggested. "He would have been about our age. He would most likely be very coordinated and good at all sports if he is anything like his grandfather."

"He knew who we were," said Nate. "I'm pretty sure of it."

"How is that?" asked Dion.

Nate replied, "Did you see the license plate on the back of his bike as he drove off? It read THX CHELSE."

"Perhaps we did bring him into our world through our conversations around his grandfather," offered Dion.

Chelsea said, "This is all very interesting, and although it sounds plausible, it is still nothing but conjecture. We may never know exactly who he was and what he was doing in our virtual world. He sure could surf, though." Everyone agreed with that.

"I got a pretty good look at that key in his hand when he waved goodbye," said Anthony. "Maybe we are turning over a new leaf in our journey, so to speak."

"This has been more than enough for one day," said Kim.

It was time to end their session in *The Lost View.*

They all took off their glasses and looked around.

They were all still in Kim's basement on Tuesday evening after school, and Victor was nowhere around.

"That was the most realistic session we have ever had," said Nate. "It was as if our real world and artificial one came together. I need to call Victor and find out what he is up to."

Nate called directly from Kim's basement with the whole gang listening in. Victor was just getting home from school due to the time difference on the West Coast. He listened to the story Nate and the others shared with him.

"This is very amusing," he said. "You say that this took place several years in the future?"

Nate nodded. "Yes, that is correct."

"You know," said Victor, "after hearing about some of your virtual reality experiences as we corresponded on the science fair projects, I got curious about these systems. A week ago, I placed an order for a pair of glasses from a new company advertising the latest technology. I know that they will not be as advanced as your experimental ones, but I figured that they would still be very entertaining and useful. I should receive them soon."

Nate said, "I am happy to hear you are well and continuing your engagement with some of the newest technology. You have always been, and remain today, an inspiration and a good friend to all of us. We just had to hear your voice after that crazy session in *The Lost View* that we just finished."

Victor replied, "Maybe our virtual and real worlds will coincide someday."

As they hung up, everyone agreed to stay in touch often as they grew into the real future, full of unknown discoveries.

Chelsea asked, "Why was the key spinning in the astrolabe during this session? I had not seen that since I was practicing for *The Caribbean Adventure*."

She recalled the experience and remarked, "That was such a coincidence. The streamer on my throne fell off during the practice session video and again in the real performance."

"Wait a minute," said Dion. "I watched that video a hundred times. The streamer did not fall off in the recorded rehearsal, only in the actual performance."

Lucia interjected, "So Chelsea, you were the only one who remembers seeing the spinning key in the astrolabe in your field of view. Maybe you had been watching a very accurate reenactment of the future through a virtual world while the rest of us were watching the recorded video."

Anthony replied, "Well, if that is the case, what we just witnessed in our last virtual reality session may be an equally accurate prediction of future events, given that the key was also spinning in the astrolabe during the experience."

"Wow, maybe you are correct," said Nate. "If so, I look forward to meeting Fred's grandson someday."

Chelsea smiled. "Not to mention surfing in the Caribbean with all my friends. Now *that* sounds incredible."

"I, for one, am glad that we are finishing up our interactions with the world of *The Lost View*," said Nate. "I like living right here in the present moment with my friends. Friendship is the most important thing to us. We have each other, something which we can all count on. We interact on a totally different level than the artificial. We are not like robots that carry out tasks. As they advance, we may never understand all that is inside of them. However, together we are capable of staggering creativity that can astonish and bewilder even our own imaginations, with or without artificial intelligence."

Everyone agreed that Nate had hit the nail on the head with those comments.

The friends had finished their assessment of the glasses. Per their agreement with Chelsea's dad, they were to write down their impressions of their experiences while using them. Chelsea remarked, "It seemed only fitting that we meet at Lake Moon Glow to collect our thoughts." The gang agreed to go there on the following Saturday morning.

It was a clear, crisp morning in late spring. All the vegetation around the lake was thriving and vibrant with color. Mating duck pairs swimming around on the lake were making a small ripple wake behind them, reflecting glistening sparks to the eye in the shape of a 'V'.

Everyone settled along the lakeshore as Chelsea started the conversation. "We ended up getting much more advanced software than was originally intended for us to receive. That led us into experiences far beyond what we had anticipated."

"That is for sure," said Dion. "It may have been a coincidence, but I think the world of *The Lost View* saved my life when I was about to cross the street that day after seeing the monarch in our virtual session. Not to mention the family on Mulberry Street who lost their house but were saved."

Anthony added, "Well, I got saved by a giant turtle that brought me to shore." Everyone laughed.

Lucia said, "It just occurred to me that the spinning key in the astrolabe that somehow looked different must have been the key design that the surfer had. The astrolabe has been used for centuries to predict all sorts of things. In ancient times, the positions of the stars were thought to offer a wealth of knowledge."

"Who knows? Maybe they still do," suggested Dion.

Lucia replied, "So the new key may hold secrets of its own. It may be easy to confuse the artificial and real worlds as things progress. The line between real and artificial is bound to get a little blurry."

Nate commented, "This is all valuable information that we should include in our report to Chelsea's dad."

Kim interjected, "What would be a good way to reminisce? Let's walk around the lake, then head up the Wandering River to relive some of our experiences in our virtual world."

"That is a fantastic idea," said Nate.

Everyone got up and began walking around the lake, reliving their experiences in the world of *The Lost View* and individually relating those experiences to their real lives. As they headed upstream of the lake along the banks of the Wandering River, they concluded that artificial intelligence could teach each of them a lot about themselves because it reflects their thought processes and those of many others like them.

Soon, they came to the bridge over the river. Anthony reenacted the giant prehistoric dragon-like creature that ate all the green slime in the lake, adding, "He must have liked 'Chopped Sewage.' He was trapped forever in this very spot, pointing to the bridge."

Everyone laughed at the silliness that was created inside the world of *The Lost View*. The gang all realized that this was just crazy made-up stuff.

As they walked across the bridge, Nate noticed something in the rock cliff bordering it. He pointed and said, "Look at the rock. Something is sticking out of it."

Lucia remarked, "It looks like some sort of prehistoric bones."

As they approached the formation, they could see what appeared to be the jawbone of a large prehistoric reptile protruding ever so slightly from the rock cliff.

"Do you think...?" wondered Kim.

"Almost anything is possible," replied Dion.

"We do not know all the secrets about the key and its blind side," said Chelsea. "As things progress, we will most certainly discover more. Our future is filled with challenges and excitement."

As Nate reflected on Chelsea's comments, he responded, "Yet the fundamental nature that makes us who we are, is most certainly preserved as a constant thread throughout history and into the future. We journeyed into a world very different than our own and experienced things that we would not have expected. And yet, in some ways, everything remained the same. Our values, friendships, relationships, desire to explore, and passion for knowledge did not change us. We learned humans could adapt in many ways but remain fundamentally the same."

Everyone joined hands and agreed to meet the next challenges head-on, whatever they might be.

"There is one thing about a shiny key," said Dion, "it always reflects the light. What we see in that reflection and what we decide to do about it is a choice we will each have to make."

THE END

About the Author

Michael J. Piatt lives in Cincinnati, Ohio. After a career as a technologist and inventor, he shares lessons learned through this book.

If you were entertained or found value in this book, please consider leaving a review. It helps immensely.

Be on the lookout for the following book in The Key Series, as the story continues.

Visit www.piattbooks.com.

AUTHOR'S OPINION

OUR RELATIONSHIP WITH ARTIFICIAL INTELLIGENCE

Artificial intelligence is still in its infancy. It is difficult to predict just how quickly it will influence various parts of our lives. There is no doubt that its capabilities will expand and continue to impact our daily lives in increasingly more profound ways. Its influence on the creative process is most intriguing.

Much of creativity is assimilation of information from diverse sources to form unique combinations that serve a purpose. An artificial intelligence system that can instantly access more information than the human brain puts at the disposal of the creator limitless possibilities for expression.

One thing artificial intelligence systems do extremely well is to bring to bear relevant information from vast and diverse sources. The human intellect can then more easily sift through this information for nuggets of genius that can be further refined for a particular circumstance. Hence artificial intelligence systems can be a catalyst for human creativity by presenting options to the creator previously not considered.

Artificial intelligence systems are facilitated by structure. Language is one such organized structure devised by man. There are a finite number of words and rules for putting them together. Hence artificial intelligence systems make remarkable correlations from this huge yet finite database. Since words are a window to our thoughts, our intellect is defined and communicated with words. Word correlation generated by artificial intelligence can have a significant relevance to us in many ways.

Like all creative endeavors, sometimes the integration of word patterns from a database is profound, at other times, they may be nonsense. One of the most important aspects of randomized correlations may be the ability to generate triggers of new thoughts that a person can further refine. Or feed back into an AI system, as an evolutionary iterative enhancement of a concept.

Another structured human sensory metric is audio patterns. There are a given number of audible frequencies. There are multiples sets of rules and structures such as speech inflection, music theory, and so forth for combining these frequencies. Artificial intelligence, armed with the huge database of audio sequences in its entirety, can make remarkable correlations that are both unique and relevant.

We as humans can do the same thing of course, but we are limited by the database of our own memory and single brain's capability. Unique audio compositions randomly created by an artificial system can evoke strong emotion and human response, just like some randomly paired words can.

Yet another area where artificial intelligence systems can excel in originality is in the creation of visual arts. Although more data intensive, images can all be represented as minute pixels and a finite number of colors perceptible by the human eye. Hence new correlations between these pixels and their color content can produce novel meaningful expressions, especially when coupled with a database of favorable patterns.

Three-dimensional sculpture, two-dimensional imaging, and time dependent videos are all candidates for an artificial intelligence system that can capitalize on known relationships between pixels or groups of such. Like vocabulary, speech, sound, and music, artificial intelligence systems can create new pixel mixes independently, or offer an artist a springboard to new perceptions. Limits to its capability are based only on the rules that lead to the correlations from the virtual sea of available data.

An artist may have a rough vision in their head of what they want to create, but often the media speaks to them through all their senses and their emotion as the work progresses in harmony with the material from which it was created. Givin that artificial intelligence systems rely upon the necessary database and rules of engagement to do the same, it becomes more of a challenge for artificial systems to draw upon inspiration directly from the media from which the piece is created.

Similarly, the other senses we humans possess, such as touch, taste, and smell are harder for artificial intelligence to replicate and act upon. This is because we do not always have well defined rules of engagement and quantifiable measurements for these senses. There are exceptions, such as beverage testing, which may be among the first to be exploited by artificial intelligence systems because the correlations of taste and smell can be quantified to some extent.

That is not to say that advances of artificial intelligence systems in all areas of human endeavor will not be forthcoming, because they will be. They will be paced only by the data available to them and their ability to learn from it. The latter being coupled to the rate of advancements in chip technology necessary to do the processing of information.

So, what is stopping artificial intelligence from becoming completely human, you may ask? Each of us is the summation of all our unique histories, including all our sensory inputs, combined with our genetics. A machine may "adopt" a set of information roughly the capacity of a human brain or greater, but it will not be making decisions the same as we do. Our decisions are based on logic, emotion, and all the complexities of life. A machine will make decisions on logic and what it can figure out to be emotion from correlations within its database.

Is artificial intelligence intelligent? It depends upon the definition of intelligent. In many ways artificial intelligence is just doing what computers have always done, which is making calculations in ones and zeros. The difference is that that over the past 75 years, its computing power has increased dramatically, along with an equal number of years of database generation from which it can draw information to perform operations upon.

Programmers independently decided on the first computer operations for our benefit. Now computers can program computers with operations based on input of only a general intent, rather than a specific set of instructions. This makes them extremely capable of many things, but not necessarily intelligent from a human perspective. We are complex beings that can act unpredictably. We evolve and change our perceptions. We define and redefine our narrative of self on a regular basis. We can adapt and cope. Both joy and grief have helped to shape us into who we are. Telling a machine, it hurts is not the same as feeling it, so the reactions may not be the same for the machine.

The influence of artificial intelligence on our lives will continue to increase, having a more profound impact on who we become. The best way to prepare for the future is to learn, remain aware, and to question. Our future is in our own capable hands.